This Way Slaughter

Other Novels by Bruce Olds

Raising Holy Hell
(Henry Holt, 1995)

Bucking the Tiger
(Farrar, Straus & Giroux, 2001)

The Moments Lost
(Farrar, Straus & Giroux, 2007)

This Way Slaughter

A Novel of William Barret Travis

Bruce Olds

Let us have madness openly.
O men of my generation.
Let us follow
The footsteps of this slaughtered age

—Kenneth Patchen, *Before the Brave*

WingsPress

San Antonio, Texas

2018

Cover art: "The Doughboy (man with bayonet)" © 1914 by Djuna Barnes
Used by permission of the Djuna Barnes papers, Special Collections and
University Archives, University of Maryland.

First Edition

ISBN: 978-1-60940-569-4 (Hardback/cloth)

E-books:

ePub: 978-1-60940-570-0
Mobipocket/Kindle: 978-1-60940-571-7
Library PDF: 978-1-60940-572-4

Wings Press
627 E. Guenther
San Antonio, Texas 78210
Phone/fax: (210) 271-7805
On-line catalogue and ordering:
www.wingspress.com

Wings Press books are distributed to the trade by
Independent Publishers Group
www.ipgbook.com

Library of Congress Cataloging-in-Publication Data:

Names: Olds, Bruce, author.
Title: This way slaughter / by Bruce Olds.
Description: First edition. | San Antonio, Texas : Wings Press, 2018. |
    Identifiers: LCCN 2017041376 (print) | LCCN 2017045072
(ebook) | ISBN 9781609405700 (ePub Ebook) | ISBN 9781609405717
(Mobipocket/Kindle) | ISBN   9781609405724 (Library PDF) | ISBN
9781609405694 (hardcover : acid-free paper) | ISBN 9781609405700
(epub) | ISBN 9781609405724 (pdf)
Subjects: LCSH: Travis, William Barret, 1809-1836--Fiction. | Alamo
(San Antonio, Tex.)--Siege, 1836--Fiction. | Texas--History--To
1846,--Fiction. | GSAFD: Biographical fiction. | Historical fiction. |
War stories.
Classification:
LCC PS3565.L336 (ebook)
LCC PS3565.L336 T48 2018 (print)
DDC 813/.54--dc23
LC record available at https://lccn.loc.gov/2017041376

For Mother,
    & in memorium, Ronald Johnson (1935-1998)
        shaman, bricoleur, cosmic thief

To the reader:

This novel is set in a time of rampant racism which the text reflects. What better antidote to the romanticization of flawed heroes than to let them hang themselves with their own rope?

"What," a cuckhold named Travis wondered shortly after having shot and killed a man in advance of riding hellbent for Tejas, "what possibly could have enticed me to this desolate country, save the wish to stay alive long enough to die here?"

When on horseback and armed with my Jaeger carbine I crossed from my home state of Alabama into Mississippi, then Mississippi into Louisiana, finally Louisiana into Texas, into Tejas, which is to say from America into Mexico, I did so in deliberate, purposeful violation of recently-passed Mexican anti-immigration laws. As such, at the moment of my having done so—and doing so was surprisingly easy owing to the border being woefully unsecured; unpoliced and unpatrolled, it was preposterously porous—at that moment I became not only what that country considered *un vagabundo*, a vagrant and vagabond, but an undocumented alien, armed outlaw and foreign undesirable of the first water.

I was then—as I recall, this would have been May of 1831—all of 21 years old, on my own for the first time in my life and all alone in what I took at the time for a Comanche-infested nowhere both unimaginably hostile and unthinkably savage. And yet, despite the risk of apprehension, arrest, detention, imprisonment, God knew what else (or perhaps the "else" was so unthinkable that even God did not know), I had little choice but to hazard whatever dangers might arise.

I had little choice because I was running, though whether I was running away or running toward was not a matter that I spared much thought for at the time; that would become clear only later, if never entirely. All I knew then was that I was running for my life, since, as it happened, I not only was an illegal alien in the eyes of the Mexican government, but a fugitive from justice in my home state of Alabama.

In short, I was a wanted man, much wanted. A wife-deserter and child-abandoner, yes, but also, more to the point, according to state law, recently passed, badly conceived, poorly considered, inconsistently observed and capriciously applied Alabama law—the very Law by which I had been making and continue to make my living—a "willful" murderer, one punishable upon conviction by death. By hanging.

Obviously, the elements of a story would seem to lurk here. Curious, isn't it, how often there seems to be one of those reposing just beneath the surface, a story, in this instance the one about how I found myself in the fix in which I found myself and to some extent find myself still. The one that involved and in some sense still involves a woman. Always seems to be one of those too. A woman I mean.

The problem, of course, is how to tell it, such a story. How to choose which version—there are so many, infinitely many— might best unlock the door, perhaps several doors, leading to the deepest understanding of what in fact occurred. And then, having chosen, having settled upon *that* version in particular in preference to each of the no less legitimate others, to tell it without resorting to cheapjack melodramatics on the one hand, or the crippling distortions of an excessive, over-scrupulous verisimilitude on the other.

The story begins, this version of it that I have chosen to *spin*, with the consequences bred of a failure of character. In this case, my dubious own; what it tickled Rosanna, my wife, ex-wife now, to describe as my "deficiency of integrity." It is a description with which I am disinclined to quibble. I will not gainsay that as a husband I could not have been a better one. Certainly I could have been more attentive, less inconsiderate, less self-absorbed, have better listened. I could have doted more.

Still, when a man, a husband, discovers that his teen-age wife, the mother of his child, his only begotten son, is fucking, or what amounts to the same thing, being fucked by someone else, someone not himself, what, that husband might be pardoned for asking, is the proper response to that? What the right requital? What are the rules then? Which conventions of civilized human behavior may in such an uncivil circumstance be said still to obtain?

Upon discovering that one not only is a cuckold, is being cornuted, but that one's wife is *with child* by another man, what, in the name of all that is holy, is the right and honorable, correct and proper, the *just* course of action to such a life-altering, emasculating trauma?

Of course there is the law as written. The letter of the law. The one on the so-called books. There always is that. But what recourse when that law and its letter fail to provide for a compensatorily proportionate remedy for the damage inflicted and injury sustained? When it furnishes no adequate means of redress and restitution, no sufficient avenue of which the wronged, utterly devastated party may satisfactorily avail himself?

It is said that we are a nation of laws, and so we may be, but sometimes—who should know better than myself, someone who makes his living, quite a respectable living, from knowing better—those laws are so much bosh. Sometimes, oft-times, the law has less to do with ensuring justice, than with sustaining a semblance of so-called civil order.

The irony—for what story, after all, what version of any story might be said to merit its telling that is not steeped in the ironical—is that I did not even love her. Rosanna. I had grown over time not to love her. If indeed I had ever loved her. (I must confess that uxoriousness is one phenomenon that always has bewildered me. As, too, that of wittol-dom.) Whether, on the other hand, she loved me, or once did, who might say? Most likely she was in love with the idea of being in love. Most women are. Most 16-year-old women at any rate.

Which doubtless accounts for why I never bestirred myself to ask why. To seek an explanation. For why she had done what she had done. Whose fault it was. Who was to blame. If it was me. Something I had done or failed to do. Because I no longer cared. I did not care to know. Because knowing would have changed nothing. Nothing worth changing.

Not that she didn't volunteer one, an explanation, after a fashion, in her own way. "If'n only you'd ever for one second lifted yer long nose outta them damn law books," she offered.

"If'n only you'd ever of loved me the way you do them. If'n only you'd ever of paid me and yer boy baby a moment's mind the way you do them words in them damn books, none of this here....."

Coming from her—well, unable to bear another word, I confess that I cut her off with a cuff. Split her lip. Drew blood. I know, I know. Unpardonable. Before, losing control completely, belting her about a bit. Black-and-blue-ing her some. More unpardonable still. In truth, I was thinking that perhaps she would miscarry, hoping that she might miscarry, praying that she would miscarry.

All considered and re-considered? She got off lightly.

My killing that man, killing—it profoundly pains me all these years later to so much as utter the name Fosterberg Williams—my killing Fuzzy Williams had nothing to do with Rosanna Cato (or, for that matter, poor Fuzzy himself) and everything to do with me. My being so affronted. Mortified. Scandalized. With my being privately and publicly disgraced. In a word, with my being so humiliated, an humiliation so entire that in order to reconcile myself to it, I had no choice—even now I feel, no choice—but to destroy utterly the source of it.

I considered it as I consider it still, a *mortal* offense.

I could, of course, have killed them both. There was a moment there, perhaps several, more than several, when I wanted to kill them both, contemplated killing them both, was perfectly capable of killing them both. Whether they deserved killing is another matter. Whether they deserved killing by my hand is, perhaps, arguable. But then, at the time, it was my considered judgment that deserved had nothing to do with it.

There was hash to settle. I was honor-bound to settle it and settle it I did. I killed him, Fuzzy. But I did not murder him. It wasn't murder. It was a mutually agreed-upon, consented-to, fair and honest face-off. Fair fight all around. Pistols. Classic duel. Code duello. Unlawful, yes. Quite so. Indisputably against the letter of the law as written. But not at all uncommon, not in Alabama, not in those days.

More's the pity, I am a crackshot. What some call a dead-eye. (Similar to having perfect pitch, so I've been told.) Which is where I shot him, in the eye, right eye. Blasted it to bone crater. Blew it right up and out at the root. Helluva piece of offhand shooting if I do say so myself. About which I feel now as I felt then, no remorse.

I am not remorseful. Nor do I aspire to remorsefulness. Not that I feel particularly gratified about or indemnified for what happened. Had to happen. Though I do, I reckon, feel avenged. To an extent. Some small, insufficient extent.

I am aware, of course, of those who since have theorized that I left the States to get out from under what they are fond of characterizing as "an Aetna of debt," and it is true that at the time I was indeed some $900 in hock, a perfectly grotesque figure. But, no. That wasn't it. Not at all. In fact, I satisfied that debt later, in toto.

I am no less aware of those who have hypothesized that I left, as they are wont to describe it, with "his docked tail tucked between his cowering legs" owing to my recently having suffered a defeat in the local courts so "personally humiliating" that it rendered me a neighborhood laughingstock. And, it is true that I latterly had lost a case that left me with considerable egg on my much mortified face. But that wasn't it either. Every lawyer loses a case now and then, and while some defeats are more difficult to swallow than are others, such losses come with the professional territory.

No. The truth is that I had in confidence been reliably informed that the order for my arrest was to be issued before the end of that court session on March 31st. And so, I left. Lit out. Told no one that I was going. Why I was going. Where I was going. To Tejas. No-Man's Land. Nearest *despoblado*. Nearest nether zone at hand. I just saddled up and slipped away. Slunk off. Skulked if you like. I have no difficulty saying skulked. Middle of the night. Up and unceremoniously disappeared. Injun-style. Cat's paw. Not a word or note of fare thee well. In farewell.

Was it difficult leaving him behind, my son, Charles Edward, my Chazzie? It was agonizing. I agonize still. But I could not take him with me. Where I was going—impossible, out of the question.

I knew like everyone I knew knew—it was then a matter of much-publicized public record, a subject bruited and bandied about in all the newspapers and much discussed in both churchyard and dramhouse—that at the official invitation and with the enthusiastic endorsement of the Mexican government which had commissioned him to cultivate and civilize its Comanch-terrorized, northern *frontera*, Stephen Austin had for the past decade had an American colony (no native Mexican could be bribed or persuaded at bayonet point to settle there) up and running out Texas way.

So that what I had vaguely in mind when I left Alabama, to the extent that I had anything in mind save shagtailing it anywhere else *muy* pronto, was that if I could somehow make it the 700 miles to Austin's colony, to its capital of San Felipe without being apprehended first, being caught up in some damn Mexican *federale* dragnet or scalped to death by a Comanche raiding party, that perhaps something like a fresh start might be available to me.

A place to start over. Turn the page. Begin again. Forget the past. Or bury it. Or, if not bury, then at least put enough distance between myself and it that its violences might eventually fade, fade and decompose of their own accord, gauze over enough to disencumber me of their more bitter memories.

This young man's foolish hope: that one might forge a future by forsaking a past.

People have told me about life in the Far-West
And my blood has groaned: "If only that were my country!"
....to live without faith or law,
Desperado! Over there, over there, I will be King!....
Oh! Over there to scalp myself of my....brain!
To swagger, to become once again a virgin antelope,
Without literature, a boy of prey, citizen
Of chance....

—Jules Laforgue, "Albums"

(Did my body make an objection to traveling
across Texas   internal conditions in which I   abstracted myself
… If a being could be the product
of a ground one tastes, then I was Texas developing)

Pivoting the desolate rim of the night world
the stars a billion diamond concho smithereens high
    as halos in my head
not enough sky to nest 'em.

Nerves dangle off my body spitting sparks
swelling sound fever swirling hot, naked
wet as acid winds.

Weather sealed sudden as sirens
steering west, always west, furtherwest, westering
emissary to somewhere.

Not a solitary soul for a million miles in ten-thousand years
saluting the night
like a flute.

Come morning, hunting evening's dinner, cross its path, or it, mine.
Kill a cougar. Carve it up. Eat off'n it, puma meat, raw and bloody,
for days.

Dawn paws through the switchgrass where I am bedded down jarred awake by a hook plunged through my neck. Brushing at the damn thing still half-asleep I knock it away with the back of my hand, watch it scuttle off bullwhip tail flicked high as a flag.

Ow. *"Fuh-uck!"*

Its barb sunk in, having snagged there, tugs, drags me in after down my throat chuting through myself sleeving a funnel of flame. Pour of yellow venom python crawls through cutglass across hot coral hissing raw red awake in every carnal coil, cog, singular cell a torch jabbing *ka-pow!* against the bulge of my neck gnash of branding iron pressed there and held, pressed there held, pressed there held, and held pressed there until my volcano head explodes, every planet in my head vomiting pinwheels, starblooms, flowerbursts, sporeblasts mushrooming blackened out my scalp helmet of seared flesh flayed to fabric bone face sheared off scalpeled away and I braille it with a hand feeling nothing, nothing there, face, brow, cheeks, nose, lips, mouth, fused smooth as slab of sirloin.

My brain is left. Apparently. Apparently all that is left of my brain is left. All that is left is what is left of my brain stuck on a stem impaled on a spine its mesh net catching every passing minnow of the language of pain. Eyes laboring leap from their sockets swimming for their lives sutured to drawstrings jerking—*zig/zag*—five directions at once crashing through chop of lunatic wave after wave in oculogyric crisis. Flannel ears stuffed full of every unsilence of a world so muffled life falls cinder-soft feathering towards a distance fetched infinitely far.

So now *Christ!* my heart is punching beserk out my chest pumping black blood everywhere, churned pitch-hot surfing my skin, mad slick of spat grease.

Downthroat past a tongue slurred to paddling lava this plunge of scalded fist closing closing closing to a claw clenching frantic air seeking channels cinched by belts pinched rib-tight buckled against my breath, every lunglift a caber heave, flexed shoulders fanspread on fire their wing-rack of flesh charred cushion for a thousand drill pins.

Lampreys of pain.

Need to piss. Afraid to piss. Have to piss. Sharks' teeth lick my leg lengths when *Jesus!* harpooned on a spit roasting inside out praying not to combust my cock flame of whale slush scorpioned at my feet.

The United States as we understand
Took sick and shat out the dregs of its land,
Her murderers, bankrupts, and knaves you may see
All middened as one in San Felipe.

Austin

I recall arriving in San Felipe saddle-sore and trail-talc'd fourth week in May, first week in June, by which time I had lost all track of time, though those there who claimed to be its keepers struck me as scarcely the last word upon the subject. (I can say now that the trip was nothing to speak of save for that single, singular Natchez Under-the-Hill night during which I had gambled and won and lost most of what I had won, though not gone so bust that I did not have enough left over to rent a woman for a slick hour—Creole as it turned out, or so she boasted—before I had again to be on my way. I can highly recommend Natchez in that respect. As such women go, the Natchez sort are both surprisingly affordable and commendably professional. Not artists, perhaps, but certainly compliant enough artisans of a certain energetic competence. They also are uncommonly clean.)

San Felipe, it turned out, wasn't much. But then, I wasn't expecting much. I had no expectations, nor proper claim upon them. At that time, I rough-reckon 500 people were domiciled thereabouts in four or five dozen log cabins as well as various lean-tos, dugouts, shebangs, shanty half-sheds and shacks, even a few canvasback tents strewn stercoricolously to either side of the single hogbacked road—the Atascosito, as I was shortly to learn—that slanted through the gridless, purposely unpatterned town. To each side of the road, troughs slickened green and ruckled with the ooze of human waste and animal refuse belched vapors foul enough to clutch the place in a frothing ripeness so assaultive it burned to breathe too deeply.

There appeared to be but a single hotel (The Pilgrim's Whiteside Rest or Roost), a single pair of taverns (The Last Shot and Marty's Last Chance Beehive), a few general stores, a schoolhouse, a smithy and wheelwright, post office, land office, and a printer's shop (home, according to the sign propped in the window, to either the *Texas Gazette* or the *Mexican Citizen*). But, curiously, not a single church. A stab had been made at what I took for a central plaza, but the Greek nymph cupid-and-cherubim-less fountain at its hub was but half-built, and that half half-bygone.

I was told upon inquiring that Austin lived "out northskirt way on Bullinger's Creek," so I decided to ignore as best I might the growlings of my voluable belly in favor of pushing straight on for the Empresario's homeplace—trailed at a wary watchful distance by a solitary, mange-ridden pariah dog of vulpine cast and lupine gait. Branching then banking then bisecting a bulge then a rise then a gap then a downslope through a stand of loblolly pine I remember off-angling toward a house I apprized through the trees as a single-story, double-wing, patchily-whitewashed, hewn-log structure technically known, I had cause to know, as a double-pen cedar plank dogtrot.

Nestled in an elaborately trenched, intricately foxholed fold of hedgerowed horseshoe glen back off a brushy creekbank, I was taken well aback to note that the structure was policed by a single four-pounder cannon perched upon a picket-rung platform nearby its entryway, as well as what I took for a pair of scaffold watch or signal towers upthrust to either flank a good 15 feet in the air. It was a layout, I recall remarking to myself at the time, not at all unconducive to defensive perimetering at a moment's spurred notice.

Austin, I quickly discovered, was home, but drastically off his feed. Or so he confided shortly after welcoming me inside his "not unhumble abode."

As we talk, I surmise that he not only is uncommonly engrossed in and by the state of his own health—apparently hypochrondriacal by nature, he enumerates insomnia, absence of appetite, "tourniquet" headache, "ill-fitted" tooth pain, ague fever and "heart complaint" among his more chronic maladies, as he does a "disposition" to grippe and rheumatism in the winter, "an agony of unlimbering come spring"—but that he is as melancholic a soul as I ever have encountered, something he attributes to having only recently lost his younger brother Brown, "upon whom I much-relied and to whom I was extraordinarily close."

Whatever the cause, he radiates an aura of world-weariness, untold burden, exaggerated gravity, even gloom, a hangdog gloom as enveloping as a fogbank, thicker than some glue. Thirty-seven years old, with his slatted sides, stooped shoulders, receding hairline and puttied pallor, he seems a fair decade older. Were he to smile, such the impression, his whiskerless face must only fissure to fractions. Laugh, and it would fall piecemeal apart. Sober, this Austin, though less as a judge, so he strikes me, than an undertaker, one clad in the drab, loamish brown and black earth tones of his frockwear as for the lackluster grave.

"You know, Mr. Travis," he says of a sudden crick-cracking his knuckles, "I am possessed of a most singular aversion to the phenomenal. And yet it dogs me sir. Hounds me day and night."

I remember being at a loss as how appropriately to respond. The phenomenal? I do not respond.

"Sins of the father," he says, "is it not so?"

Is it? I have no idea. "Well," I say, needing, I feel, to say something, "my own once sired a bastard son. Taliaferro. To his credit, did right by him, pa did, took him into our home, schooled him, so on. Ma's permission of course. Tally, he was reared no differently nor suffered unduly."

This, it would seem, falls upon deaf ears. For all that my reply appears to register with him, I might better have kept silent.

"My father's name, as you may know Mr. Travis, was Moses. Fine name, I suppose, though I venture he took it too seriously. It was his idea, you know, all this Texas business. I never wanted any part of it. But then he up and died, his dying wish being that I carry on in his stead. So," he outspreads his arms and glances wide about, "here I am having in the meanwhile fallen hopelessly in love with that which I curse as often as not."

I recall distinctly that our parley did not last long, an hour at most, if time enough to learn that he lives alone, has never married, is outspokenly, even maniacally anti-religionist, fluent in Spanish and consistently formal and decorous, if neither officious nor punctilious in deportment and manner. At one point inviting me, "Tell me about yourself, Mr. Travis, as much as you are comfortable telling," I do so, pleading that there is not much to tell, save that which needs remain untellable.

"Ah, yes, of course," he says, slowly nodding his head. "The past is past. Wipe clean the slate. *Tabula rasa.* Fresh start. You will find many here, most perhaps, who are cut from quite the selfsame cloth."

Between sniffles he informs me that he is at present deeply involved in actively lobbying for repeal of Mexico's recently enacted Anti-immigration Law which he considers, "beyond injudiciously detrimental to what we are endeavoring conscientiously to accomplish here, an act of the sheerest folly," although he allows that, "as we Texians presently outnumber our *Tejano* counterparts some eight to one, a disparity that grows only more disproportionate by the day, it is perhaps understandable that the government in Mexico City should, going forward, wish more assiduously to monitor its *frontera norte.* The demographics are all on our side."

After having me sign the "certificate of admittance"—mine is No. 588—that officially registers me as a "colonist, bachelor," entitled to legal claim on the standard quarter-league land grant of 1,107 acres, "the location of which with certain exemptions is entirely up to you," he admonishes me to learn, "with due diligence and expedition," both the local law and native language, before adding, "and if you must prioritize the two, Mr. Travis, you will do well to choose the latter. Learn *Español*, son, for in this country, *este país*, you will go no further than it will carry you. *El idioma es la clave.*"

Snuffling, the Empresario dabs some at his coryza, then licks his bowstrung lips across which no smile is permitted to flicker.

Everything he says, each po-faced, deadpan word, at a minimum every other word, is wrenched from a mouth downdragged at its commissures beneath a pair of Abyssinian brown eyes drenched in rheum; when he tilts his head and the light catches them at a certain glancing angle, they appear almost…aubergine.

When I ask after the prospects of setting up a law practice, he is quick to recommend a spot called Anahuac—he pronounces it "anna-whack"—a town apparently some 100 miles due east on Galveston Bay that apparently serves as Texas's official port of territorial entry. There, he suggests, where the government in Mexico City has established a customs house and garrisoned a monitoring fortress, "a man of your certain talents and obvious ambitions is, as I am given to know, not only much needed to represent the interests of the Texian citizenry there, but would have the field, as I understand it, the legal field I mean, much to himself."

Massaging his temples with calipered fore and middle fingers, he cants his head then squinches his eyes the while palping first clockwise, then counterclockwise, first left, then right, before pressing the heel of a hand to a hinge of jaw, and wincing. "We are not yet splendid, Mr. Travis. As you can only have noticed, we are not yet resplendent here. But neither are we as abject as we may appear. We are on the rise, sir. Fear not. We are rising. And should you be of a mind to rise with us, then Anahuac…" Leaving off mid-thought, he pauses, cocks a brow. "Your indulgence sir, but—I hesitate to ask, is that … scent?"

I remember smiling at this. "Well, intoxicant, intended to be. Lavender and…"

"Bergamot!" he exclaims.

It is at that moment that I decide to like Austin. He lacks a certain vitality, true. Suffers from both an excess of austerity and paucity of charisma. Is perhaps too susceptible to self-pity and complaint. But while he is neither the warmest nor backslappingest man in the world, he more than compensates for the deficiency with a commendable lot of gentlemanly couth. And hygiene. Despite his hypochondria, perhaps on account of it, he is hygienic. A man who is himself hygienic can detect that in another man. And to discover it out here in the rough-and-ready, wild-and-woolly, middle of no-damn-where, how not respond favorably?

Sensing that I am overstaying my welcome, I am about to take my leave when he favors me with "the speech," the same he has over the past decade made, I assume, hundreds of times:

"Mexico, Mr. Travis, as you will discover soon enough, and forget only at your peril, is decidedly not America. Here, men are not created equal. Here, they are granted no god-given or inalienable rights. Here, they may pursue their happiness, but only up to a point as determined by the government. Here, they may worship god, but only as the state ordains. Here, there is no writ of habeas corpus or trial by jury. For that matter, there is scant local autonomy of any sort, and the doctrine of personal property is but a matter of public expedience. *La Autoridad*, the Mexican Authority, can be manipulated to your advantage, but only within discrete limits, and even then that manipulation must remain as often as not a matter of silence, subtlety and slyboots.

"Understand, son, that this is a country yet in its infancy, one yet to grow up and hair over. It is a country whose constitution is barely seven years old. A country that achieved its independence from its motherland a scant 10 years past. A country that still is to discover what it is, what it stands for, what it wants for itself, has yet to establish an identity of its own, and that these facts taken together render it oft-times too feral of flesh and raw of nerve, fearful and uncertain, oversensitive and prone to irrationally taking offense and sensing hazard at every hand.

"We all are possessed of our private aspirations. What part yours may have played in your decision to come to Texas, I do not know. Nor do I need to know. What I do know is that whatever they are, they are unlikely to be realized in just the way you might have imagined, or"—grimacing, he clutches at his chest—"may be imagining still. Not that they must be disappointed, only that"—jaw-clench, chin-jut—"Texas has a way of, how put it, revising, if not dismantling them altogether.

"This is not to discourage you, nor ought you be discouraged. For those like yourself, young, ambitious, sound of body and mind, nimble of resource and wit, the opportunities here are boundless"—lip-gnaw, neck rub, shoulder roll, &c—"so long as you are prepared to maneuver within the rules of your new reality, rules that in time you will learn can be bent, if less often broken to your benefit.

"And so, Buck, here is my most earnest counsel, and you ought feel free to dispose of it as you may see fit. All that you may assume you know, all that you may believe you understand, all that you are convinced your experience has taught you, everything you have been and are at this moment, is from this moment *en peligro*, at hazard, subject to a re-becoming, a reinvention that, however unnatural or contrary you may find it, is for now beyond your capacity to conceive.

"You will discover, son, that the signs of unfriendliness, if not outright hostility, are everywhere. Be observant, discreet, tactful, vigilant, learn in silence to read them, and only then respond. Appropriately. Accommodatingly. Find it in yourself to do that, and I am confident that you not only will prosper, but discover in Tejas your destiny, whatever that may prove to be."

These, I recall thinking at the time, are well-considered words, words that I intend as I may find myself able to avail myself of them, to heed by heart and soul and mind. In light of which, I know too well, I will in the event be needing to place a tether upon my temper. I will needmost to bank my fire, the one that flares and flames of its own accord more often than even I might prefer.

"*Y ahora, buena suerte, Señor* Travis. *Buena suerte y vaya con Dios.*"

Penny. Pound. It's all in for Anahuac.

"*Giddap!*"

A Belated Prolegomenon

The chronological truth of one version of the story, which is to say the *mischgedicht*, warts-and-all one that we soon shall be about excavating here, had its genesis with the Louisiana Purchase circa 1803. This being, it merits mention, half-a-dozen years prior to William Barret Travis's birth.

Under the terms of that legally dubious, 15 million dollar transaction with France, then-President Jefferson understood the territorial rights of the United States to extend to the *Rio Grande*, while Spain, then Mexico's colonial mistress, contested such a (mis?)understanding, contending that those rights extended no further than the Calcasieu River in present-day Louisiana.

For the next 15 years, the territory between the Calcasieu (the "Arroyo Hondo" to the Spanish) and on westward to the *Rio Grande*—essentially present-day Texas, then little more than a desolate frontier inhabited by marauding bands of Indians (so remote and precarious is this *frontera norte* that native Mexicans refer to it as *el lugar más allá del mundo*, "the place beyond the world")—remained between the two countries the source of ongoing dispute, intermittent friction, and, on occasion, open conflict, outright conflict distinguished by a series of so-called filibustering expeditions (from the Spanish *filibustero*, meaning "freebooter"). These unsanctioned paramilitary forays launched from American soil were aimed expressly at wresting Tejas from its Spanish/Mexican owners in order to establish it, in time, as an independent, slave-holding, rogue republic.

The bloodiest of these forays, popularly known as the Gutierrez-Magee Expedition, occurred as early as 1813 when a force of some 1,400 republican filibusters, covertly supported by the U.S. State Department, was routed at the Battle of Medina just south of the town of San Antonio de Bejar by a

Spanish Royalist army commanded by one General Joaquín de Arredondo.

Prominent among the General's officer corps was his protégé, an 18-year-old lieutenant named Antonio de Papua Maria Severino López de Santa Anna y Pérez Lebron, who subsequently participated in the mass hanging of 800 of these bootstrap filibusters, as well as a Tejas-wide pogrom of rape, torture and beheadings carried out against their putative civilian supporters. Brute and brutal times.

While American citizens had begun "squatting" in significant numbers on Tejas land as early as 1815, it would not be until 1819, under the terms of the Adams-Onis (or Transcontinental) Treaty, that Spain and the United States mutually agreed to fix the international boundary at the Sabine River, the latter nation, in effect, relinquishing its claim to the disputed territory. Instead of settling the matter, however, the treaty only exacerbated it. Indeed it was that very summer that yet another filibustering foray was undertaken, this time numbering some 300 men, among them a 23-year-old, Kentucky-born Louisianian named James Bowie.

Throughout the decade to follow, especially after Mexico gained its independence from Spain in 1821 and eight years later constitutionally outlawed slavery, the U.S. government made repeated, if uniformly unsuccessful attempts to purchase the territory it had once considered its own and unabashedly continued to covet.

Mexico, meanwhile, frustrated in its efforts to encourage settlement and economic development of its vast (270,000 square mile), if equally inhospitable *despoblado* (depopulated zone), and powerless to stem the burgeoning flow of American emigration, endeavored to control and contain it by authorizing certain "reputable" individuals called *empresarios*—the first and most prominent of whom was Stephen Fuller Austin— to *"siembre la tierra,"* seed the ground by establishing the immigrants in so-called colonies subject to Mexican law.

(Austin's alone comprised some 15,000 square miles.)

This, it before long became apparent, was tantamount not only to inviting a skulk of foxes into the henhouse, but, owing to the natural rapacity of the species, of serving it chicken dinner upon a well-burnished platter.

Nonetheless, in the United States, the 1819 treaty remained an object of widespread scorn and derision. Not only did such prominent slave-owning senators as Henry Clay and Thomas Hart Benton bitterly denounce it while lobbying for its abrogation, but the Federal Surveyor, William Darby, characterized it as "a monumental and egregious blunder worse than folly," predicting with uncanny prescience (in the *Nashville Clarion & Tennessee State Gazette*, 4/6/19) that:

"No artificial lines will operate to stem the torrent of western emigration. The laws of nature will be neither arrested nor thwarted by a roll of parchment. The increasing and restless men of the west will follow on regardless of future consequences. Why the United States should relinquish a part of its domain, I cannot see, and still less can I see the sense or policy of adopting an order of things which inevitably must produce savage war."

By the time William Barret Travis entered the territory a dozen years later, that savagery waited only upon heedless hap to erupt with all the force of bayonets.

Such, then, the frame, ground and context.

Anahuac

I do not wish to dwell upon my Anahuac Experience. Pointless, not to say distasteful, it involved a matter, a decidedly unpleasant matter, that until now I have been reluctant to discuss.

Notwithstanding, in the name of fair, frank and full disclosure, I feel honor-bound now—for if not now, when?—to place upon the record to the best of my recollection certain facts as I, and I alone, was privy to them. However painful and humiliating to me they may have been and continue to be, the version of the story that I have vowed to tell renders the registering of those facts not only necessary, but of the utmost moment.

It has been said, or perhaps I am the one to say it, that a passion for the inevitable is the last honor of defeat. And this, on the face of it, is a noble sentiment, one that as a Southerner and a soldier makes to me not only perfect sense, but resonates to my soul. In this instance, however, this Anahuac instance, as well as all that followed and continues to follow therefrom, there necessarily is more, much more, that shouts for its saying; it is that which I intend to say here.

Now, as singularly down at the heel as I had found San Felipe, Austin's colonial capital was by comparison to what I discovered at Anahuac, a veritable clinquant city on a hill. Even as I approached on horseback, while still a good mile from town, I was slapped full-brunt across the face by a wave of air so noxiously thick, high and sharp that my eyes began uncontrollably to water. (Can eyes bristle? Air fester? Can an odor, a *mal*odor, claw?) So much so, in fact, that I was obliged to brush away the blur of tears with the back of a wrist while yanking my kerchief up over my mouth and nose clean to its bridge.

It was, I learned soon enough, a stank that emanated in part from the neighborhood's interlocking maze of raw sewage sinks, coupled with the rankish rot off the seagrass-meadowed bay, the inordinately shallow Trinity Bay with its oystershell-middened shoreline littered with tens of thousands of dead fish (cat, drum, gar, skate, bowfin, mullet) and hundreds of diamondback terrapins broiling belly up in the sun, the lot apparently churned and chucked there by the hurricane that had rip-sawed through the country from Galveston but a fortnight past.

The only inn in town, as Austin had advised—if a crazy-quilt of thatch-roof, wattle-and-daub *jacales* and a cannon-heavy, brick masonry *presidio* perched atop a 30-foot-high pigsoil bluff overlooking the bay merits the descriptor "town"—was J.W. Hardin's. (The proprietor, so the rumor, was the same who had murdered a man back in Maury County, Tennessee; such rumors, such being the unspoken local custom, destined to remain rumors). So it was there, at the heart of what I was to learn was called *El barrio norteamericano,* the American Quarter, that I put up for the duration in a draughty, windowless, if not uncapacious room that I did my best to makeshift that it might double for a serviceable office space.

Most of the 50 or so Anglos living in the Quarter, despite the insularity of their often clashing political allegiances—some few, I discovered, were for Texas independence at once; significantly more were for it at some unspecified point further down the road; a fair number were content to abide if not embrace the status quo ("Live quietly and go about your labors in peace, harmony and concord" being the prevailing wisdom among these "Tories"); some, most perhaps, were a middling muddle of mixed feelings and conflicted convictions—were possessed of a legal status not unakin to my own.

Among their number was a name that, along with a letter of introduction, Austin had back in San Felipe been so generous as to furnish me, and so my immediate order of business was to track down one Patrick Churchill Jack who, excluding myself, was the only lawyer then on premises. Bespectacled, bacon-faced, the bandylegged Paddy C was, as Austin had described him, a "bantam rooster of a man," a short-tempered, brashly outspoken, native Georgian less than a year my senior who long since had ceased being in the least self-conscious about the *nevus flammeus*—the size of a fighter's fist—that laid, wine-dark, along his lower jaw.

Having been directed to and finding him in his rooms a scant street or two over from Hardin's, I was immediately warm-welcomed inside where Paddy poured us each two fingers of rye whiskey—I am not partial to spirits, but thought it only neighborly in this instance not to spurn the gesture—before easing around to what he referred to as "certain matters of imminent moment."

As he related to me, it had been but a few months prior to my arrival that Paddy apparently had run afoul of the town's Mexican commander—the same Austin had admonished me to steer well clear of owing to his being "perfectly incompetent to such a post, too much of a jackass to be governed by reason or judgment, and when not half-crazy, a consummate fool"— when he too openly sought to raise what he called The People's Committee of Civilian Self-defense, Safety & Protection, a sort of ragtag, Anglo-only militia unit "armed and minute-ready."

"We had to do something," Paddy explained. "It is no secret, though none could in good conscience, Travis, fault you for questioning its credulity, that half the 200 Mex *soldados* here, these so-called *presidiales*, are convicted felons, not a few of them rapists. Indeed, one of them, a black-hearted murdering swine named García-Ugarte, is the commander's own personal secretary. Shocking, is it not? No! What is shocking, is that here, in Anahuac, it is not—shocking. Not shocking in the least.

"There is a document, official document, I own a copy— nor was it, you may believe, come by cheaply—that it would benefit you to familiarize yourself with sooner than later. Entitled *Reglamento de Presidios*, the 'Regulations for Presidios,' it contains the clause, I quote, 'Regular garrison forces shall be composed of vagrants and other disorderly and disreputable persons who shall be recruited by entrapment and decoy.'

"Appalling, is it not? That such a practice should be the official policy of the government, any government? What is more appalling still is that such scum not only is permitted to roam the town here at drunken, carousing will, subjecting the good citizens of this community, including our women, especially our women, to the most profane verbal abuse and intimidating physical harassment, but that despite our repeatedly bringing such wanton outrages to the attention of the ranking officer, no finger is lifted effectively to remedy or so much as curb or mitigate them."

Targeted as *cabecilla*, Anglo ringleader, Paddy had been arrested—it would not be the last time—before being hurled, hooded and Lilly-cuffed, into the brig of a Mex schooner anchored in the bay. There, it was duly explained to him that: one, the assembling of such an independent armed militia as he had organized expressly contravened Mexican law—"a fact," said Paddy, "that being neither illiterate nor entirely unversed in their language I knew damn well, it being so stated under their fucking Article 26 of their fucking so-called Military Law"— and two, as matters of defense "are strictly the prerogative of the commander of this garrison and no one else, you will in the future abstain from all such traitorous activity while bowing to his legally constituted authority short of which not only will you find yourself confined aboard a ship bound for Matamoros where the Commandant General will dispose of your fate, but your fugitive rabble will find its collective neck bent beneath the imposition of the harshest strictures of a stern and unforgiving martial law," including curfews, detentions, weapons confiscations, search-and-seizures, 24-hour street patrollings, &c."

"The commanding officer here...?" I began.

"Bradburn. The worst sort of tyrant. Sees enemies and conspirators everywhere—or contrives them wholecloth.

Hallucinates saboteurs; conjures provocateurs, outside agitators, infiltrators, instigators and trouble-makers; imagines agents deployed *sub rosa* to frustrate and undermine his every decision. Conceives of anyone who would dare raise a whisper to question his judgment or protest his authority, much less lift a hand actively to oppose or resist it, *'un enemigo del estado,'* an enemy of the state.

"Guilty. We, all of us here—now yourself as well, Travis, you would be wise to understand—are in his eyes guilty. Of what? Who knows? Of our presence I reckon. Of having the temerity to walk with him the same earth and breathe the same air, acts which he construes as an affront to his imperial authority, an authority he is authorized by his superiors to exercise unchecked. Welcome to Anahuac, Buck."

"I see. But the *civil* law here…"

"Takes a backseat to the military. Defers to the military. Is superseded by the military, or rather, by its principle of *fuero militar*, which renders it exempt from all civic authority. Not that it matters. The ass refuses to recognize our right to practice it, much less to contest its particulars in court, at least the ones that might apply to him and his thug command. Calls us cornstalkers, canebreakers."

"Pardon? Cane…"

"Lawyers absent legitimate legal standing. That we practice without *una licencia valida,* a valid license, one that only Mexico City can confer, but never has, not to a non-native born applicant. Ever. No, as far as the law is concerned here, Bradburn is lord, master and sole sovereign executioner, and we are but his geldings."

Removing his eyeglasses, Paddy fished a handkerchief from his breast pocket, flapped it free, and fell to polishing what I previously could not help but notice were their uncommonly thick lenses.

"Have you," I ventured, "thought to appeal to Austin? Could he not be persuaded to intercede on our…"

"That was done. That occurred. A meeting did take place during which Austin voiced our concerns, as he likewise advocated suspension of all these ridiculously onerous tariffs and excessive custom duties the Mex slap on our American cargo vessels. In response, so Austin assured me, Bradburn vowed both to more conscientiously respect the civil authority here and more assiduously monitor the behavior of his troops. Instead, the scoundrel continues to recognize no authority save that of his military superiors in Matamoros and Mexico City while the depraved effrontery of his men grows daily only bolder and more widespread.

"Anahuac is not San Felipe, sir. As it lies outside the boundaries of his colony, any influence Austin may wield here, any pressure on our behalf he may bring to bear can be effective only as it stems from his status, reputation and genius for diplomatic suasion.

"Which is to say, it is not binding. It perforce lacks tooth. And nothing could be clearer than that such tooth, sharp tooth, *colmillo*, fang, sir, is what is most sorely required."

Fishhooking the templetips of his rimless spectacles one behind each ear, he rose from his chair and crossed over to the Congo African Grey squawking on its perch, withdrew what appeared to me an unshelled palm nut from his weskit's pocket, and relinquished it palm up to the parrot's talon-grip upon which it, the bird, fell instantly more silent than a birdless sky.

"No, it is all on us, Buck, and us alone. We are endowed with our certain godgiven rights, and whether Bradburn and Mexico City choose to acknowledge them, they are inalienable. Should we fail to defend them in the face of those who would dare trample them to dust, we shall only deserve that which we are bounden to reap."

I must have known it was coming. Yet when it came, the vise-crunch of that psittacine beak, cracking the nut like a gunshot, I must confess that I started and ducked while Paddy roared with delight until the tears flowed, his glasses fogged, and I cursed a streak so blasphemously blue, I dasn't repeat it here.

When you know a language, you know a people, and when you know a people, you know their world, at least as much of it as may be knowable, and such knowledge, while a guarantor of nothing, offers the possibility, slim as it may be, of shedding some available light towards illuminating a beginning. A place to begin. To be. Some common ground. A way, perhaps, to wedge a way in. To have a haven. Even inhabit a home.

And so, in the weeks, then months to follow, there was the challenge of *la lengua, el Español*, an impediment that, as Austin had counseled, I undertook with Paddy's help to overcome, if never entirely to master. His willingness to share with me both his Spanish to English translations of certain articles, clauses and sub-clauses of Mexican civil and military law, as well as his running compilation of a number of the more commonly used Spanish idioms, idiolects and colloquialisms, and his incessant pounding of the vowel sounds—a=ah, e=eh, i=ee, o=oh, u=ooh— was at the time nothing short of invaluable.

In time, I would find myself wondering whether had such bi-lingualism been the shared verbal coin of the realm, had each "side" in the conflict to come only better grasped the nuances, inflections, and modulations, oblique allusions, abstruse meanings and opacities, implicit subtexts, leitmotivs and tropes employed by the other, whether events might have evolved somewhat...differently. For certainly, when one is deprived of the capacity to express oneself with a sufficient degree of clarity, when one cannot rely upon the existence of a reciprocal, mutual verbal and written understanding, one cannot help but feel—as was the case with myself until I had acquired a sufficient working knowledge of "the tongue"—at sea, *a mar*, a *pescado* out of water where not a *ballena* beached upon a far-flung foreign shore.

Not to make more of it than it may merit, but if knowledge is power, and obtaining that knowledge depends in large part upon possessing and controlling the language, then to have limited or imperfect or no access to that language, is to be rendered less empowered, even emasculated. And when one feels that way, one may in consequence feel not only vulnerable, but conjure threats that, however baseless or misapprehended, too often are met with expressions and gestures of a certain hostility.

I am not suggesting, please, that all differences, fractious as they were, toxic as they were, could have been peaceably adjudicated or harmoniously reconciled *if only*. Some of those differences, as I was coming gradually to understand, were too deeply entrenched, too ingrained ever to be resolved short of some measure of coercive nastiness.

The slavery issue, for example. Mexico's having legislated the abolition of the practice two years before not only had been a brazen assault upon our property rights—the market value of a decent chattel typically fell between $500 and $1,000; for most, a lavish, even exorbitant sum—but posed a mortal threat to our economic future, our cotton, cane and tobacco planting future. Which bore, in turn, upon the very reason so many had expatriated to Tejas in the first place: land. Cheap, affordable, arable land, and lots of it.

At a time when the going rate back in the States was $1.25 an acre, here it was 12½ cents. The price was irresistible, and in most it fed a hunger so rapacious that, as Stephen Austin later would remark to me, "It is with land as it is with religion, Buck. It throws otherwise perfectly sane people into all sorts of convulsions." (And speaking of religion, while Mexico City's demand that we were as émigrés legally bound to swear fealty to its papist church aroused its share of resentment, owing to the policy so seldom being enforced, most of us simply chose to ignore it. Still, it rankled.)

While I cannot say that I ever was so land-fevered myself, I certainly had my share of professional doings with those, James Bowie chief among them, who were. Indeed in my experience the attitude of the typical Texian émigré was that he would by fair means or foul acquire for himself grant title to as much of the country as he could persuade his lawyer to finagle, a predatory, unapologetically avaricious attitude that did little to endear him to his hosts.

Such thornier issues aside, there were, in my estimation, any number of others that might at least have had a fighting chance of being hashed out, sorted through and settled to one degree or another, absent the indiscriminate bloodletting that so regrettably ensued.

Often, not always—I am perfectly aware of the pitfalls—but often enough it is the disgruntlements and differences, even the deep disagreements and disparities, the *rifts* that are possessed of the potential, given time enough and world, to foster mutual understanding, if not eye to eye agreement.

What, after all, was the argument against getting to know one another at least a little better, somewhat better, before we started annihilating each other?

I heard screaming, but I was too late. I happened upon the outrage too late.

I was on the return leg of my nightly circumambulation about the Quarter, shillelagh in hand, when her shrieking, then her moaning and whimpering, as well as the growling in Spanish, drew my notice to a lonely, moonlit-stippled side lane where with some difficulty I was able to delineate the silhouette of a figure crouched over one significantly smaller sprawled upon the ground.

Helpless at that point to do much by way of intervention but endeavor verbally to calm, comfort and console the unthinkably young, understandably hysterical victim—whose name, age, height and weight, hair and eye color and distinguishing birthmarks I am with-holding here out of a sense of common decency—while physically restraining her defiler (name DeJesus, rank corporal), it quickly became apparent that the *soldado* was so besotted that such fight as he was capable of summoning amounted to little more than a britches-around-the-ankles, headlong charge.

Following a moment or two of slapstick-like lurching about to regain his balance in order to steady himself for another lunge, when he launched himself at me yet again, he collided flush with the gnarled knob of my cosh, its impact—I heard the THWOCK!—catching his skull high across the temporal, its wafer-thin so-called squama. Upon which, not bothering to so much as crumple, he went down as if poleaxed, stove-in head rooster-tailing blood.

What happened next remains something I cannot account for even now, for it happened so precipitously, it had happened before I could fully grasp that it was happening even as it happened. As if out-of-nowhere, suddenly swarming down the lane I beheld as if in a nightdream a torchbearing crowd toting buckets of what proved to be hot pine pitch—the tar, I recall it occurring to me at the time, could only have been fetched off one of the ships anchored in the bay where I knew it was employed in the blacking of hemp rope and the caulking of bulkheads and hull seams.

Jostled by the mob, for it bore all the clamjamfry'd earmarks, rudely to the side, I could only watch as the inert, drunken wretch laid out flat as a fluke upon the ground was roughly stripped of each striation and stitch of his uniform, outer and under alike, which, tattered and torn, were then put to the torch. Still out cold, more naked than the wound from which he continued copiously to bleed, he was then by the bucket-toters slathered by intermittently replenished tarbrush scalp to sole even as others in their turn spat upon the body which had quickly become the object of a roundelay of well-aimed bootkicks that I confess to having found less appalling than apropos.

Still, none of it was very pretty, as justice can sometimes be. So *basta ya*, I recall thinking to myself. I believe I have seen quite enough. Seen too much. All of a bellyful. And so, peeling off, panthered out and away, on the walk back to my billet resolving, consequences be damned, that I would in the morning submit a formal written brief of complaint and protest to the *commandante* demanding not only that this DeJesus, should he survive, be turned over for criminal trial in civil court, but that henceforward those under his command either be ordered to absent themselves from the Quarter or that he immediately recognize our right to re-establish our armed Committee of Safety & Self-defense.

Now, with respect to *El Commandante* Bradburn, I had up to that point been content to bide my time while attending to what a lawyer in such a place as Anahuac typically found himself attending to: drawing up wills, writing mortgages, certifying and transferring land titles, taking depositions in estate matters, preparing powers of attorney, filing for collection of notes, composing petitions, warrants and subpoenas, other mundane mind-numbing paperasserie civil and suchlike &c. Heeding Austin's counsel, my commerce with Bradburn hitherto had amounted to little more than the perfunctory tip of the hat in seldseen passing, typically while he was out gamboling his brace of fierce-looking dogs.

But this rape, I found myself thinking, was hardly some random, localized atrocity, an aberration that had occurred anomalously out of the misbegotten blue. No, it was, so I surmised, the result of a *systemic* failure. It was the wholly predictable culmination of an *official* policy, one that had been hatched years before within the hallowed chambers and hushed corridors of the country's *El Palacio Nacional*, a policy arisen of Mexico City itself, one that tacitly or otherwise not only tolerated, but condoned and sanctioned such vile insult to *all* Texians if only by failing to enact, institute and enforce measures to deter where not prevent it, or, once it had occurred, hold the culprits legally accountable.

Because who at last on *our* behalf, we Texians' behalf, was keeping such accounts, or cared enough to do so? All of which, every point, I fully intended to enumerate in the finest detail in my legal brief.

I am asleep or nearly, teetering on the verge, its brink, wee hour, deep night, about to drift, plunging swamped inside my nightshirt, sweating moonlight, when comes a rapping at my door that in truth is less a rapping at than a banging on followed by a bashing against as if in forewarning of a barging through, the lot punctuated by words barked over-loudly in a language that I by now understand too well: "*¡Abierto, pendejo! ¡Cabrón! ¡Abrase en nombre del Commandante Bradburn!*"

I quickly lost count of how many days I spent stripped naked and staked strap-by-shackle facedown to the floor of, of all things, a brick kiln. Beehive kiln. Brick beehive kiln. Surviving the while on little but boiled *frijoles*, moldy *pan*, feculent cod chunks and rancid, fever-ridden *agua* spoonfed me by my guards.

Fifty days? Sixty? At least 50. Possibly 60. Probably 60. Fifty to 60 days confined in chains, unclothed, prostrate inside a darkened, low-ceilinged, dust-choked room, a damn athanor not much larger than a larder infested with mosquitoes the size of scorpions and scorpions the size of manta rays.

The kiln, or *horno, horno de ladrillo*, was located just south of the fort, all but camouflaged on one side by rushes, reeds, willows, ferns and cat-tails, and on the other by cane, hemp, bamboo, raffia, sisal, and, I might have sworn, rattan and jute. Actually, there were two such kilns, an unmatched pair, the larger of which the Mexicans designated Hidalgo, the smaller Moreno. I occupied the latter, but both were favored with a single, loaded, inward-facing cannon.

It was summer. I sweltered.

By turning my head, I remember, I could with some contorted rubbernecking just glimpse the cannon out the kiln door. Its blackened iron bristled with sweat.

I am permitted to micturate and defecate twice daily using a crude chamber pot more akin to a slops bucket. Lidless. Scarce leakproof. Emptied only when having begun to overspill across the floor. I am permitted to neither shower nor bathe. I am not permitted to shave. I am provided with *chicle* to chew instead of tobacco, which, the latter—unclean, sumpy, repulsive habit—I eschew chewing in any case.

I am permitted to sleep through the night slackened some if not entirely unchained. I am permitted *un tramo*, a stretch, 15 minutes in the morning, another 30 in the evening—*gracias, muchas gracias*—to uncramp my cramped muscles. I am permitted no reading or writing materials. I am permitted to sing, to whistle, to rave as it may please me to do so, however theatrically.

Once a week, I believe upon the Sabbath, I am raised by rope pulleys above ground in the center of the kiln space and my genitals and arse are not ungently washed: jostle, tug, outspread, rub. This occurs, I either remember or am imagining or remember myself imagining, at the dandling hands of anonymous, silent women of a certain age.

It is a regimen of sorts, a routine. Funny what one clings to, comes to count upon in such a situation for a measure of predictability, some semblance of order. In time, little else to do, I become so proficient at distinguishing among the several rats that overscatter my cell at night, that I am able to identify each by their signature repertoire of bwips, pips, peeps, chirrups, chirps, churrs, squeaks, shrieks and screeches, hisses, foofs, chatters and chitters, whines, grunts, clicks and bruxes. My hearing, fine-tuned now to the music of rats, the scat of rats, and the rest of me to the rat-quickened dance of my entrails.

Because otherwise all you have is time. The vacancy and vastness of time. Which quickly becomes the enemy. Always vast, always vacant. And this vast vacancy weighs. Weighs more each day as it accrues and accumulates, seems to replicate, self-propagate, in any event to mount until the sheer heaviness of it begins to crush—spirit, soul, sanity alike. I resolve not to let it crush me. Not that I am uncrushable, not at all, but if I am to be crushed, I much prefer that I be crushed upon my own terms, insofar as I may avail myself of them.

That night, the night of my arrest, I had been seized by force of arms from my room while still half-asleep, unshod and clad in nought but my sodden nightshirt, in advance of being hauled—absent warrant, statement of charges or word of explanation—before *El Jefe*, before Bradburn.

Toothpicking absently at the seams of his unnaturally white incisors with a manicured forenail, he sat slouched if not unsmartly uniformed behind his headquarters desk flanked by his matching pair of *perros*. His dogs. Bandogs. Presa Canarios. 250 pounds of verdrino brindled, direwolfish beastdog, their hornless heads massive as oxen.

An abbreviated version of what then ensued, might go, have gone, now goes (more or less in English):

"Travers, is it?"

"Travis."

"Yes. I believe I may have heard of you. Lawyer. *Un abogado.*"

"That's correct."

"No, *cabrón*, it is not correct. You have no license. You practice illicitly. Without credential. Had I the authority, you may believe that all of your hell-spawned ilk, all you *escoria subversio del bien común*, all you scum subversive of the common good would long since have....Well, another subject for another day perhaps. For now, while I am under no compunction to do so, permit me to tell you, cornstalker, why you are here. You are here because actions beget consequences, violent actions beget violent consequences, and violent actions committed by interloping *gringos* against native-born members of this country's military beget—well, be assured, you shortly shall apprehend."

A globe much the circumferential size of a medicine ball, slightly smaller, perched upon his desktop. Appearing to contemplate its wheelygigging as if desiring to send it whirlybirding round and roundabout, he chose instead to leave it unspun in its mounting, a silent static rebuke to every earthen orbit. Then, leaning further in, he glanced wistfully, such was my impression, at the spheroid still frozen stockstill in place. As he did so, he sledded the right angle of his cocked elbow far-to-near across the desk while addressing the ceiling as if it contained constellations.

"What needs to be impressed upon you, canebreaker, indelibly impressed, is that nothing that happens here is permitted to happen save by my leave. Nothing occurs here save at my behest. Nothing exists here save by my sufferance. Nothing coheres here save by my consent. Nothing, nothing at all survives here save by my decree. This universe, Travers, *mi regimen y dominio* is mine, all mine, mine alone. I am its **axis mundi**. I am my own sun and about it I revolve—(here he did indeed send the globe spinning)—sworn to its heavenly, sacred defense."

I recall being surprisingly calm, my temper held, altogether *tranquilo*.

"¿*Y estupro?*"

"Eh? ¿*Qué?* What's that?"

"You say that nothing happens here save by your leave? Fine. So then permit me to ask, does what happens by your leave include rape?"

At this, he visibly reddened, face, ears, neck, and when he next spoke, he did so with words sprayed with spittle the remnants of which, settling, soon caked white at the corners of his mouth.

"What it does not include, *cabrón*, is the likes of you taking it upon yourself to beat a Mexican soldier, a professional soldier sworn to uphold the laws of the Supreme Government, to defend with his life the honor and integrity of *Madre México*. What it does not include is caning one of **my** men, **my** command, *comatoso*."

How he had come into possession of this information, how he was able to pin the initial blow on me, I was never to learn. Spies, perhaps. Or informants.

"And your evidence?"

"That is none of your concern. What is your concern is that you now find yourself in *un mundo la mierda*, a world of shit. What is your concern is how an *insurgente*, an *insurrecto* such as yourself, once having been bound over to a military tribunal on the charge of treason, the penalty for which is plain, intends to face the everlasting wrath of his Maker."

This, I recall thinking to myself, was all so laughably predictable. And then, I did indeed laugh. And then, he was shouting.

"We are done here. Guards, take him away. Remove him from my sight. *¡Fuera de aqui!* Out! *¡Ahora!* Deliver him to Lieutenant Montero. *En los hornos.* At the kilns. Deliver him to The Keeper of the Kilns."

Insurgent, he had called me. Insurrectionist. Enemy of the state. Subversive to the common good. And do you know? Perhaps I was. Perhaps by that point, that is precisely what I was. Perhaps that was what everything I had seen and heard and experienced over the past several months had left me little choice but to become.

Because Bradburn? All said and done? Bradburn was the least of it. Bradburn may have been an insufferable ass, a petty tyrant, he may have rapped a few knuckles, split a lip, blackened an eye, loosened a tooth or two, he may have threatened bastinado, but Bradburn, for all his obvious defects of character, was not depraved. He may, as Austin had intimated, have had no business commanding a garrison, much less one the ranks of which were weeviled with perverts and prison convicts, he may have been a perfect incompetent, but he was no deviant. He wasn't pathological. He did not prey sexually upon the powerless and imprisoned.

The brick-kilned.

His lieutenant, Manuel Miguel Montero, on the other hand…

Not every night, but over the course of my two month confinement often enough, this man who was less than a man, other than a man, would slip into the kiln under cover of darkness. Masked. Always masked. A masked man. Ritually masked. A mask of pliable black leather that smelled of leather. A black leather helmet mask that covered his face and head save eyes, nostrils, and mouth. But I knew. I knew it was him. He made no secret of his identity. To the contrary. He would whisper it in my ear.

"*Estoy* Montero," he would whisper. Or, rather, whinny, nasally whinny, whinny so near deep into my ear that the hot, fecal stank of his *pulque*-soaked breath would dizzy me.

"*¿Usted nunca olividara, eh gringo? Cómo vives usted siempre recordara mi nombre.*" In other words: "I am Montero. You will never forget it, eh gringo? As long as you live, you will always remember my name."

He just liked wearing this mask, apparently. Perhaps he wore it in the event that he was caught in the act. Or perhaps he believed that it concealed his identity from his papist god. Perhaps he just liked the way it smelled. Who knows? I never understood that part of it, frankly.

Also, a fact meriting mention, he never failed to tote with him this whippet-thin, flexible cane whip. And a knotted ball gag of cotton batting.

Well, you can imagine. Perhaps you cannot imagine.

Perhaps you prefer not to imagine. The pawing and fondling and licking, earlobe and neck-nipping, the probing and inserting and penetrating and so forth, followed by the whipping—which typically left me much reddened and extravasated but uncloven of flesh, for he clearly had done this before, many times before— was a bit much, if nothing I could not bear. Nothing that could not be borne. Or so I told myself in-between muffled screams.

I was defenseless, of course. Could do nothing to defend myself. Maneuver or move self-defensively. Move at all. Twisting, writhing, bucking, thrashing—all equally pointless. As was asking why or saying no or cursing or crying out. I could not cry out. I was gagged.

In time, one learns what one circumstantially must to survive. One learns to cease resisting without submitting. To relax but not surrender. To accommodate but not reconcile. To keep oneself to oneself for oneself. That hardened core of interiority that at bottom, at floor, remains capable, available, of being kept.

Hardly a laughing matter, though Montero was himself a warbler, quite the giggler, much given to giddy outbursts of be-spritzed and girlish giggling. High-pitched, girly giggling. I can still hear it. And the stank of him. I can smell it still. His reek. And feel it. The wet of him upon my backside.

When I consider it now, it seems not only a dream, but an implausible dream. If it hadn't happened, happened to me, if I didn't know better, I would not believe it myself. But it did. It did happen. Just as I have described it. This truth, sordid truth, a truth, as the truth so often is, that is unaccountable. Unaccountable and arbitrary and impossible.

And nonetheless, true.

What happened next, although as I was still kilned at the time I remain to this day somewhat hazy as to details, was my rescue, followed by my release and eventual repatriation.

Initially, I assumed that it could only have been Austin who somehow had succeeded in persuasively pulling enough of the right diplomatic strings to win my freedom, but this proved not the case at all. No, apparently, so I was to learn later, what had in fact occurred was that a veritable riot of armed Texians from Austin's colony numbering some 300 strong and led by one Robert McAlpin Williamson, had surrounded and laid siege to the fort, the *presidio*, until Bradburn was compelled not only to relent, to capitulate, but to take to the bush, hightail it under cover of darkness from the vicinity altogether. Those boys had wanted his head on a pike and, had they been able to run him to ground, would have had it.

Despite my best efforts, the fate of his beastdogs, I was, regrettably, never to determine.

During my imprisonment, I had resolved that should I somehow escape or by some other means be freed—not that I counted upon the likelihood of such a miracle occurring—I would leave Anahuac and return to San Felipe, throw in my lot, such as it might be, alongside Austin, seek my fortune for good or ill there. I badly needed to get away from the place. I could not remain. I hadn't the heart Paddy did. Mine was too gouged.

First though, first and last, so I vowed to myself, I was bound and honor-bound, should the occasion arise, to see, however long it might take, to the tying, everlasting tying, of a certain still dangling, lunatic loose end.

The garrote, procured in the event from the saddlepouch of one of my liberators, was a hank of stiff, slender twist rope of some 18, 20 inches. Shorter than a romal, longer than a quirt, I had artfully knobbed it at just the right irregular intervals with rough, tight knots, hard as pebbles.

I had while confined often imagined slipping up behind him in the dark. Or let us instead of him, rather say it. Behind *it*. Close enough to tap *it* on the shoulder: "May I have this dance?" Smooth as ice. Silent as stars. The same ones that it shall, I know, shortly be seeing.

I had been rehearsing this scene for months.

So that when the time arrived, I could not feel my heart thumping. Did not hear the bloodrush in my ears or jangling of my nerves. My palms were dry as chalk, my hands steady as a jeweler's. My breathing regular. My throat and lips moist. My knees strong. My stance right-balanced, lock-firm fast.

My thoughts were...I believe I had no thoughts. None that I recall. I believe my mind was blank. A blank. White as whitewash.

I was as alert as a coil. That I do recall. I remember thinking, "*Soy cobra.*"

So what are you waiting for?

The flash-move is silent-smooth. No whoosh, no ripple. My upheld left hand clutches one rope-end just behind its right shoulder as my right fast-loops the other up, over and around its head on its left-side, arcing across in a semi-circle counterclockwise.

Upon which I *yank*. Both directions. Opposite. At once. Right and left. Hard apart. I have by my ordeal been weakened. Now I am suddenly strong. I summon the strength both available *and* unavailable to me. I yank and continue yanking, hard as I can.

Its arms fly up to its neck. Its hands claw at the taut, tautening, tautened rope. Too late. Its body bucks this way, then that, thrashing. I hear it gurgle. Pig-snort. Spray spit.

It tries to twist its head, to wrench it, arms flying back behind its head trying to reach, grasp, grapple, trying to grab hold, get at me.

I yank harder. Then harder still. I redouble my yanking, reckoning that right about now its eyes are beginning to bulge out of their sockets, its tongue blackening, protruding fat as a toad between its bluing lips.

I reckon that its trachea is slowly being crushed as I feel, then hear something give. A structure giving way. Crumpling. Crunching. A cartilage. I reckon that its lungs are burning up. Combusting. That its heart is fixing to burst.

And then it plunges, but in increments, to its knees. The arms drop slowly, then fall quickly to their sides. The head lolls, droops, nods and pitches forward, chin-point upon chest. Slack. Limp. I feel the tug of the whole weight of its sag against the rope, befallen.

Motionless, soundless. Unmuscled and unbreathing. Undone. Deadweight. Dead meat.

And it is then that it defecates. Or perhaps it had done so earlier, but I had failed to notice. I smell the smell only then.

So keep yanking. Harder. Tighter. Another minute, half-minute, a minute or two more before I let go. Unwind the rope. Let the body fall. Its carcass. Let its corpse fall facedown to eat earth.

No more keeping now. No more kilns to keep.

And then turn, turn and without a word walk rapidly away, thinking—I suddenly realize that I am thinking, that my thinking has resumed without my thinking about it—"It makes you wonder, what kind of bother is death? What kind of mess is involved on such occasions? Self-made mess. Man-made mess. And life, really, little better."

Turn and walk away thinking to myself, about myself: "¿El Verdugo, eh hombre? Soy, El Verdugo."

The Executioner.

I am, throughout, not wearing a mask.

(...in Mexico, as the horizon when you are
moving can oppose the horizon inside...
a style that has got the future wrong.)

For what they may be worth in their recounting—I suspect not a lot—my dreams—and I take it that they *were* dreams and not visions or hallucinations—my dreams during the period of my imprisonment, as for some while thereafter, remained curiously non-descript save for several degrees of gyroscopic tilt and temporal warpage possessed of an uncalibrated register and range of catch-as-catch-can discontinuity that saddled me with a sense of being my own pluperfect assailant.

Does any of that make any sense whatever? Need it?

Perhaps I can be clearer. What happens in such a situation, at least what happened to me, at least as best I can recollect it, is that one...shrinks. Constricts. Shrivels. Balls up even as one feels oneself emptying out. That is, one's reality does. One's reality comprises naught but a diminution, a shrinkage inside oneself, down into oneself, as if into the very narrowed marrow of one's own deepest dreamt, self-devouring bones.

Oddly enough, I seldom dreamed of my mother or wife or child, neighbor or colleague, friend or enemy, or any recognizable person familiar or otherwise. Or when I did, if I did, I did so most unvividly, even evanescently, as if steeped in claude glass.

Brute Nature either.

What this might be said to say about me or the state I then was in I hesitate to remark beyond assuming that I indeed was, at that time, in such a state, being myself not entirely present, save, of course, figuratively. I could not say where I was materially, corporeally, in point of concrete fact. Or even if I was. For I seemed to have lost track, all such knack.

Asleep perhaps. Dreaming perhaps. Out of body perhaps. A figure of vapor perhaps.

Difficult to get out of one's own way at times, one darts off so quickly, so obliquely that one stubs one's toe upon one's aberrant absence at every vagrant turn, held as one must be at arm's length against oneself.

In any event, *not there*, direct, specific, tactile experience of that sort, the violence in my left haunch for instance or locked crick in my neck, being, while shackled, either unavailable to me or happily deferred or detoured, i.e. entirely lost, but not wholly gone, one being *of* but no longer *in* the moment as those moments followed contiguously, if no longer sequentially much less chronologically, each upon the next.

(Generally speaking, things can, I like to believe, be said to occur in the right order, or at least *an* order, or where they do not, can be emended and revised later by memory to constitute another version that may better accord with said haphazard and deranged disarrangement. This is especially true as it pertains to torture and self-torture.)

Insofar as this begins to sound like madness or some semblance thereof, that is because when one finds oneself in trouble of a certain dire and "unreal" sort, precisely the sort I found myself in while kilned at Anahuac, and one discovers that that which is "real" fails to provide a solution to that trouble, or even some little relief, one has little option save to seek escape and refuge in that which is not real or less real or even unreal as a more useful, effective and, ultimately, sane alternative, the real having proven itself not only useless, not only chimerical, but altogether inimical.

Sometimes, when one is in extremis, say, the truth is that the truth is most useful when its truth is eschewed. This might be characterized less as vanquishing or triumphing over it, than dissociating or disassociating oneself from it, since its purpose always is to tear time in two. Or, as I often thought of it during those interminable two months, to "push the pain away," something I intermittently was able to accomplish by repeating to myself the mantra, *Fear of death is the ember of life/Fear of death is the ember of life/Fear of death* and so on ad infinitum.

My dreams, as I recall their factual content, perhaps I mean fractal content, or what masqueraded as such, adhered over and over again to the selfsame pattern of composing and then hideously dismembering themselves; besides being perfectly unpeopled and arrestingly uneventful, they were likewise absent recognizable location or ground or depth of field or concretized context or frame or framing device, as they were bereft of all quiddity and sense of quiddity, whether that of the occasional unraked vacant lot or recently raked-dry and riprapped gulch.

My breathing, shallow as it increasingly was, was smoothed to visibility, gray as grisaille across the surface of a mirror while cupping a hummingbird in my hand, perhaps to afford it a measure of respite from the ice floe fragments flowing— some few blued in shimmering seafoamed flotillas—along a pitch-pined peninsular lakeshore at first light, even as some undesignated embouchure bone-whistled up a sleighbelled storm to no apparent purpose.

Such conjurations, you may believe, were suffused with neither guilt nor regret nor shame. None, at least, that was palpable to me. Only confusion as seamlessly uncontoured as a face effaced of its features. No object, no image, no definitive image of object, no objectified image, only untethered abstractions manifested as a sourcelessly random yet apparently compulsory plunge or slippage—triggered by seizure? convulsion? transient stroke of some sort? In any case, an immersion amidst a free-floating, free-falling chaos buoyed day after day by an attitude of *non-acquiescent* **acceptance** whilst staked s—p—r—e—a—d eagled spangled in flame, even splurged in it (as I literally felt, at moments, moments as fraught as they were unforgiving) within that airless coffin of a kiln. It was an immersion, thank god, in which for a few brief moments here and there I was able to LOSE myself, pump myself clean as rinse water, baptismal water white as albedo, as, to remain even marginally sane, I found I so often was obliged to imagine it.

Meanwhile, in my fading in and out moments of cruel lucidity and pellucidity, at least insofar as I still was capable of mustering them, I could only pray, perhaps foolishly, that it someday might yet be possible to live something like a dignified if not entirely meaningful life despite the indignity upon indignity I was suffering and suspected I would, once released, continue to suffer.

Certain damage, once done, cannot be undone.

This is all I wish to say and will be saying about my "kiln time," about my dreams and my dreaming and/or non-dreaming of them. Altogether necessary, perhaps, but singularly unpleasant.

Dreams are tough nuts to crack.

C.V. : Episteme & Doxa

Name:

William Barret Travis. Cognomen, "Buck." Acquired upon being thrown from his horse as a youth. Less familiarly, "Will." The middle name, Barret, being the phonetic analog of his paternal grandfather's surname, Barrick or Berwick.

Birthplace:

Mine Creek, Red Bank Community, Edgefield District, Saluda County, far-western South Carolina, some 20 miles east of the Georgia border.

Birthdate:

August 1, 1809. Eldest of 11 children of Mark Butler Travis described as "a perfect scoundrel, a rogue and rounder, rake and roué," and Jemima Stallworth, who reared him according to the dictum: "We are free to do nothing, save what we must."

Education:

Sparta Academy, Conecuh County, Sparta, Alabama (grammar school). McCurdy Academy, Monroe County, Claiborne, Alabama (secondary school). "Reads the law" under James Dellet, head of the Claiborne bar, to which he is admitted, February 1829.

Wife:

Rosanna Cato. Married, October 1828. Age 16. Separation, April 1831. Divorced ("spousal desertion"), January 1836.

Fiance:

Rebecca Cummings. Betrothed, April 2, 1834. Age 24.

Children:

Charles Edward. Born, August 1828.

Occupation:

Teacher, McCurdy Academy. Owner and editor, Claiborne *Herald.* Attorney-at-law, Claiborne and Gosport, Alabama, Anahuac and San Felipe, Texas. Land-owner (7,000 acres in East Texas). Slave-owner (he prefers "lifetime indenturist") of Ben, Jared, Jack, John, James, Simeon, Eliza, Callie, Joe. Colonial Secretary, Austin's Colony. Commander, Texas Volunteer Cavalry. Colonel, Texas Regular Army.

Religion:

Christian, Protestant (baptized Baptist; in Texas, member of Caney Creek Methodist Church), anti-sectarian, anti-papist. Publicly deplores, "the Catholic superstitions that infect the daily lives of the impoverished and ignorant peoples of Tejas," and denounces "the priestcraft as it is practiced in this country as little better than witchcraft, though more harmful and corrupt."

Description:

Height, median. **Weight,** middling. **Build,** medium. **Eye color,** a midmost blue that "bounds and bounces yet bonds." **Hair color,** a spongy ginger possessed of nutmeggy cinnamon highlights, but of a body and texture so ungovernably topsy-turvical and insubordinately whirlaway, so fraught with squally, slipshodden surges, convulsive swells and involucred, convolvulous, jack-in-the-box eruptions, that it requires superintending by a thrice-daily currycombing into an extravagantly pomaded, aspirationally precipiced quiff or gradiently scaffolded escarpment. **Dentition,** transpicuously mediocre, though neither malocclusive nor incisorally resuscitative. **Complexion,** mildly mottled, though less splotchy than spider-veined, yet not so bungled as to appear pocked or pitted, dysplastically moled or lentigined. **Musculature**, by any measure sufficiently sinewy i.e. thewy. **Ossature**, contentioned and cuttled, if oddly spurred and notchily gnarled. **Nervature**, synaptically tensile. **Metabolism**, in its high intensity strivings to keep pace, decidedly spotty. **Voice**, when lifted in song a yaargh-inflected "Irish tenor;" when spoken in casual conversation a resonantly mid-range, mint-julepy drawl muddled through with spriggy if semi-drizzled non-rhotic half-tones less lubriciously leisured than frankly honeydewed; when projected in a courtroom or before a crowd wont to a gargly hoarsening. **Habits**, immoderately moderate save for whoring, gambling (cards, dice, darts, faro, ponies), dancing, trading in expensive horseflesh and affecting bespoke, dandyish clothing. A "regular" reader of newspapers and books (Scott, Donne, Blake, *Don Quixote*, *Le Morte d'Arthur*, the Bible—particularly the Book of Revelation which he has committed somewhat to memory). An "obsessive" diarist, journalizer, log-and-ledger keeper, chronicler and letter writer who prides himself on his "calligraphically exquisite hand."

Personality/Temperament:

Quoting a self-reflective excerpt from his diary, an entry titled <u>STOCK-TAKING</u>: "I can be overproud, even prickly, though I am seldom boorish despite being unpleasant as circumstances may require or insulting as a person may merit it. If I am sometimes too slow to laugh or quick to stand on ceremony I am not entirely humorless. If I am quick to ruffle I am no less quick to smooth back. Irascible but not querulous; bumptious but not quarrelsome; intemperate but not petulant; brusque and abrupt but not combative; blunt but not imperious; aloof but not condescending; impolitic but not ill-mannered. Certainly I am ambitious though less for material wealth than the respect, recognition and approbation of my peers. I am conscientious to a fault in the discharge of my sworn duties and professional responsibilities though I may appear so guarded that others think me secretive and conniving. In my person I am uncommonly clean and fastidiously neat, even immaculate; a veritable Tartar, I cannot abide muss. While prey to bouts of earnest over-seriousness and solipsistic brooding I much enjoy a good time, having fun, even an occasional spot of prankishness and horseplay. I certainly am no natural leader of men, having neither that knack nor any aspiration to it. So many of them, those whom one would lead, whom require being led, I find frankly ill-bred, uncouth, vulgar and not to be abided in proper company. (Reading back over what I just have written here I am not pleased. The portrait, while honest enough, is far from flattering. Indeed it strikes me as that of a rather thorny and sharp-elbowed fellow, one slightly superior if not snobbish, exacting though not priggish, self-involved though not uncaring, and, all in all, significantly flawed and fallible. Much a mixed review. And so I resolve now to redouble my strivings to overcome my many shortcomings, address my several deficiencies and attend assiduously to my failings, not only for my own sake, but for those of others. In this, I wish me good sir, godspeed!)"

Three-legged Willie

The sodality to come, as the propinquity I was to enjoy on account, I never could have conceived of much less anticipated. To think, once I was back in San Felipe, that I would find myself feted, the toast of the town, a *cause celebre*—if one shortly to have a $1,000 Mexican bounty slapped upon his head—one clamoured after not only to deliver speeches upon this or that neighborhood stump, but to write for public consumption about my Anahuac experience, was as unexpected as it was gratifying. For weeks after my return I found myself unable to walk the streets without being accosted by one well-wisher or another insisting that he be permitted to stand me a drink.

The piece I eventually submitted and that subsequently appeared in the Brazoria *Texas Gazette*, the San Felipe *Telegraph and Register*, and the New Orleans *Louisiana Advertiser*, while not my own in every tittle and jot—no editor who ever lived ever managed successfully to resist the impulse to improve upon that which requires no improvement—was far from my most concinnous, but looking back, I am satisfied that it was the best of which I was capable in light of the circumstances at the time. To wit:

> The unpardonable humiliations suffered during my jungled night of the famished soul I was obliged in darkest despair and strictest isolation, not unlike the Apostle, manfully to forbear. Save that where St. Paul was by his jailers permitted parchment and quill, I was by my wardens told: '¿*Usted desea escribir, eh? ¡Luego escribe, cabrón! ¡Escribe en la tinta de su sangre en su paredes manchadas de sangre! ¡Y cuando eso se seca, en su mierda!*' (You wish to write, eh? Then write, bastard! Write in the ink of your blood upon your blood-stained walls! And when that runs dry, in your shit!)

And so on and on in a similar vein for perhaps another half-dozen paragraphs before I concluded with:

Stand or fall, we Texians must do so on our own. It is the duty now of every individual to protect himself, that self which is subject legally and constitutionally to no power on earth save his own, his <u>sovereign</u> self. Countrymen, open your eyes! Awake! *Audaces fortuna iuvat. Fortuna audax iuvat. Fortes fortuna adiuvat.* Fortune favors the brave. God smiles upon the righteous. To the victor the fruits of his freedom. Tejas! Tejas! Tejas! Tejas right or wrong, swim or sink, win or lose, live or die.

It was shortly after the article appeared that we received the news: Anahuac Garrison had been disbanded, its troops evacuated. A week or so later, more news still: the fort had by the locals been put to the torch.

Having scared up temporary digs in town at Peyton's Place, a dollar a night bed-and-board for myself and horse, I was awakened that first morning back by, of all things, the sound of a banjo. Couple, three rooms down. Someone going at it, strumming *furioso* while singing in a voice employing the vocal technique known as melisma along with a good lot of howling, growling and a stomp-holler, bucket-top scream or two.

Slipping out of bed coiled in a blanket, grabbing up my mouth harp, I dragfooted my way down the hall in bleary-eyed search of the music-maker. Which, auspiciously, is how I was to make the serendipitous acquaintance of the man who was to become my fast confederate and closest confidante in Texas, Robert McAlpin Williamson, the selfsame responsible for having secured my freedom in Anahuac. Though no one, I soon learned, called him Robert McAlpin. Or Robert, or Robbie, or

Bob, or Bobby. Or, for that matter, Mick or Mac or Alp.

Willie. Everyone called him Willie. Behind his back, some called him Three-legged Willie, *de Tres Patas*, though never Pegleg, to his face or otherwise. He did not have three legs, of course, but his right one, right leg, was bent back, locked permanently in place behind him at a right angle, frozen at the knee, stuck that way forever owing to a consumptive condition he called, "the white-swelling," a galloping infection of the bone and joint that, "bit up and rusted them out," when he was 15. Odd-looking for a fact, that wayward withered limb.

"I was laid up, bed-ridden all of two years," he confided once we got to know one another better, onto friendlier.... footing. "During which, nothing else to do, I read. The Law. On account, passed the bar at 18. My folks shot the moon trying to fix it, hinge it back aright. Nothing worked. Oil of hemlock, camphor, croton oil, tincture of iodine, syrup of chimaphila, poultices of arnica and lobelia. *Nada*. Paralyzed. Stove up. Good as dead.

"Got so eventually I couldn't *stand* it. Fetched myself out of bed whooting like a damn ape for the pain and set to juryrigging this here contraption I'd been cogitating on while I was a-laying there. A sort of pegleg. Buckle-up, strap-on number close-fitted at the knee covered with this here detachable half-a-pantleg." He winked then. "So whaddya think?"

"Two heads better than one," I said, "three legs better than two? Why the hell not?"

"Jape it gives me a leg up, foot in the door. Never known it to fail. With the lassies I mean. They're curious, get to wondering what it would be like with, so on. Truth is, I'm living with the pain each hour of every day. Don't gripe on it, no point, nothing I can't *stand*, but that dead ol' hank hurts dreadful every time a blue norther kicks up. Whoo-e!"

Which is when I reached over, lifted the curtain of his half-a-pantleg. "Mind?"

"Not a bit."

I rapped the wood, what I took for wood, with a knuckle. "So what is that? Cork?"

"Cork*wood*. Lightweight. Easy on the lugging. Weathers like a champ. Won't rot or mold, warp, attract insects or vermin, waterproof, fireproof, and, best of all, quiet as clouds and nigh as cushiony. Compared to the cedar—used cedar for the prototype—it's right enough plush. Still kick a man's skull in though, hit him right."

"So you...."

"Sure, there's sawbones try talking me into letting them cleave it off. But why? I'd miss it, miss it the way you'd miss your own dog. Nah. Think I'll stay whole awhile longer. Besides, getting carved on that-a-way? I'll pass on those odds, thankee kindly."

"But doesn't it, I mean, there must be times...."

"Heard it all my days. He won't be able. Can't do this, can't do that. Well *that's* a damn lie! Mind, I'm not like to win a footrace anytime soon, but everything else? Riding, shooting, picking the banjo, pattin' the juba and slapjazzin', fornicating? Not a hindrance. Of course, I've had more than a decade of practice at it, but a man can get used to most anything, I've found. Human animal's an accommodating creature, Buck." He winked. "Can be. Sets his soul to it."

Dimples when he smiles. I found his barely detectable lisp endearing. His breath was sweet as sassafras.

Turned out, save for the extra leg, we were much the same person, so much so I found it, not disconcerting exactly, but disarming, and I seldom am disarmed. From the moment we met, we found ourselves sharing everything—rubbish or wisdom, hard truth or lie, riddle or unpardonable slander, high farce and low comedy. We fought about nothing, disagreed about less, least of all, the more astonishing still, women.

Each, it quickly became apparent without the need to speak of it, would have given his life freely, unquestioningly, even gladly for the other.

His home place, Milledgeville, in Georgia, was no more than 70, 80 miles down the road from my own in South Carolina, we each had passed our respective state's bar at that same unheard of early age, and while he had set foot in Texas four years before me, becoming in the meanwhile San Felipe's first *syndico procurador*, its first prosecuting attorney, he had fled there for much the same sad reason, a duel fought over the dubious affections of a damn fickle woman (though unlike myself, he was fortunate enough to have only wounded his adversary in the thigh). Moreover, he likewise had labored as a newspaper editor (of the *Texas Gazette* and the *Mexican Citizen*, failing, as had I, no surprise, to eke out a decent living therefrom.)

The difference in our temperaments—Willie's was tons lighter, breezier, more footloose than my own (this was someone, after all, whose beehive beaver hat boasted dangling from its backbrim nine polecat tails)—did not prevent us sharing similar proclivities. We both gambled for higher stakes than we had ought, appreciated the fine pure blood of a fine high horse, were unabashedly partial to damson preserves, scuppernong jam, shoofly pie and apple pan dowdy. And, needless to say, enjoyed the company, at least as we could afford it, of the fairer sex.

Whoring with Willie often culminated in what he called a "whangdoodle," or "whambanger," more commonly known as a *menage a trois*. I had never before in my life, never so much as contemplated it, although I soon discovered that on such occasions, tequila helped. Sometimes. Not that I ever have been above a little debauchery as the impulse might arise, but unlike my good friend, I do not live for such moments, nor do I fancy walking around purse poor on account. Willie though, Willie was insatiable. Dr. Johnson once remarked that no man is a hypocrite in his pleasures; certainly that was the case with Willie, twice over.

And, of course, we both were "Austin men." Our politics, insofar as we were possessed of such, were an expression of our loyalty to that man, to Don Esteban, to whom we both owed so much, as in those days did every manjack in those parts.

Uncommonly companionable, Willie and myself, enough that when we decided at my suggestion to double up at Peyton's, to share a double room, "batch it," it set certain tongues to wagging, or so I was told later. Willie was aces as a room-mate. Let a man sleep in, brought him breakfast in bed, didn't snore or hog the covers or travel violently beneath them. Bathed regularly and with tension-easing aromatic (spikenard) bath salts. Trimmed a man's hair and side whiskers. Other kindly perfunctions boon and bosom.

I helped him with his seizures. Extracted the swallowed tongue.

In time, in light of all that was to transpire, it got so I was convinced that Robert McAlpin Williamson, despite wearing his epiphytes like epaulets and bromeliads like buttons, could only have been placed squarely upon god's earth to save the bacon of William Barret Travis. The first time, of course, at Anahuac, but also, later, when those *Federales* come a-hunting me that summer looking to collect their thousand dollar bounty, it was Willie, no other, who stashed me out of harm's way up north with friends 'midst the high and uncut.

And finally, during those last doomed desperate days, last hours, it was him, it was Willie alone who gave enough of a good goddamn to make the only good faith effort to effect my timely rescue.

In the seminal absence of terror we bend as if born to the bias, bloom pitched to the light towards those most like us, in the direction of our best blending. So God bless Robert McAlpin Williamson, God bless Three-legged Willie who did his dead level best to save his own fast friend. And though in the end he failed, as any man not a god was bound to fail, God bless him, even so.

Mother

I have been told that my mother's first words upon my birth—she fashioned herself something of a "foreteller," my ma—her first words as she held me bunting-bundled in her arms—as her first of eleven I apparently did not come easy; near killed her, strong as she was—her first words were, "Born godless, this one, to an early grave." Which, think about it, sounds more like a curse than not, no?

"See them furrows there? His forehead all bunched up waffle like? That there's a sign of a powerful curiousness and confusion. Wonderin' why he's here, iff'n he ought be, reckonin' on it and not likin' much what he's comin' round to. We all got us our cross to bear, but this chile here, he's like to clumb on up there all on his own. For the view, likely. Or the nails."

If life has taught me anything worth the being taught, it is that a man does well to listen to his mother. I did. Always did. I listened. But by the time I *heard*, it was too late.

Of my father, I have scant memory. It was my mother who reared me up.

Opened my eyes, there she was. Heard something, it was the sound of her voice. What I should pay attention to, what I should know, what I should love, it was my mother who vetted me along. Barely literate herself, she was the one who put some fine books in my way, who encouraged me to find inside myself whatever might be there to be found, to spend more time alone, on my own, to listen more clearly to what my heart had to tell me, what my thoughts whispered me, how to be myself within myself, all of myself without fear or fail or falter.

"You reckon who you are," her wisest words to me, "who yer bounden to be, then you be that, all of it. You be more."

Throughout my childhood, part of it anyway, shank of it, I had difficulty sleeping. Falling asleep did not come easily to me. Apparently sleeping was not in my nature. Hit the hay and there I lay, antsy, forfeit to a forever-long night. At some point, apparently, I slept. Apparently the effort entailed in trying to obtain sleep became so fatiguing that I succumbed. I never could recall the moment. I slept without knowing that I slept.

Not that I tossed and turned or drifted off only to start awake. My sleep, once asleep, was not troubled. But my mind. My mind was too…charged. What is the expression? Rarin' to go. It was, apparently, incapable of respite or arrest, caesura or quietus. It remained…on. Not on fire, as it were, but fueled. It kept thinking without my permission, as if it had a mind of its own, one that I had little to do with, over which I had scant say.

I do not recall my thoughts racing, running away with themselves hurtling headlong. I recall them swarming recursively in place, each pursuing the next round and roundabout to no enumerated end. These thoughts as hornets within the hollow of their hive, busy with their brazzing, the content of which I no longer can conjure. Just thoughts, the motion and velocity of thoughts. Their onslaught.

If only there had been something, some one thing that I could not have thought, that it would not have occurred to my thinking to think about. There wasn't.

Often, thinking to flee them, needing to, thinking I needed to flee them, I would ladder down from the loft in the dark, spider-nimble, steal barefooted across the dirt floor, unlatch, crack open and slip sidewise out the door and into the night. And then…run. In circles. Clockwise, counterclockwise, clockwise again. In silence. Silent revolutions round and round across knap of ranunculus, cowslip and rye, feet herbal and yellow-stained.

We had on our palustral property a lilypadded, viridescent millpond, and I would run rutilantly around it through marshmud and mossgrass and clumpsedge, stupidly oblivious to copperhead and cottonmouth while preternaturally attuned to the bovine sounds of the beasts billeted in our barn, the burble of our brook in its bed, the bullfrogs and barn owls talking each to the other across the heady fragrance of bougainvillea and jasmine, azalea and honeysuckle.

Moon, no moon, stars, no stars (although when there were stars, I recall conceiving of each as a bejeweled and sparkling thought), rain, no rain (although when there was rain, each drop, likewise), hot or cold, I ran. It wasn't sprinting, just a nice, steady pace to find and fall into a rhythm—and the rhyme within it, the rhyme inside that rhythm as well—that helped run the thinking out, run the thoughts away, thought to unthought to non-thought. Running thought to ground, into the ground, burial ground. Running its cerement ragged.

Slumber? What was that? Where was it in me? Each night, mystified, I wondered: am I the only one in the world, the only soul alive so afflicted, so lost to thought in the night, held hostage by the exhilirating darkness of thinking?

Lost child adrift. Young soul unsung. Sleep now. Hush, child. Sleep.

He began keeping his diary in earnest that September of 1833 as, quoting a prefatory passage therefrom, "a form of architecture, an ARK, I won't say casket, but a 'built-nest' patched of words intended to preserve certain of my memories, lest they be lost, with as much **unadorned facticity** as my pen can muster."

Following his death, the document fell into the hands of the Mexican Army until—the "chain-of-custody" in the interim remains a matter much contested—those portions of it remaining intact found their way back to Texas and the archives of that state's university in Austin where access to its *available* contents was severely restricted on a closely monitored, "need to know" basis as determined by university officials.

A few of its earliest entries:

Chingaba una mujer que es cincuenta y seis en mi vida.
(Sept. 26, 1833)

[Translation: "I fucked a woman, the 56th of my life."]

Chingaba la Suana que es 59. (Nov. 7, 1833)

Chingaba la Juanita que es 60. (Dec. 2, 1833)

Chingaba la C que es 61. (Dec. 19, 1833)

Chingaba la Mariana que es 69. (Jan. 22, 1834.)

Prospering, thriving, flourishing, save for this fucking *venerea mala.* Six months on the mercury cure; no change. But the practice booms. Clients abound. Have hired a bookkeeper, taken on an apprentice. Own six horses. As many chattel. Raising bees, farming fish, planting orchards and gardens. I may have met a woman. (Feb. 2. 1834)

Becca

I only knew him those two years before he went off and got himself killed. Murdered. Massacred. Martyred. Which, by the way, was just his way.

Us Cummings was one of the First Families. "The Old Three Hundred." Original settlers, founding settlers, the ones Mister Austin brung in to seed his colony. Made us feel like some brand of Mayflower royalty. First Pilgrims.

My best recollection, we arrived in '21 or '22; come on down from Kintuck. "We" being my bachelor brother John, my widowed Ma Rebekah Russell, my brothers, James and William, and my sister, Sarah. Settled in at Mill Creek on the Brazos. Arroyo Palmetto, Mex called it. I would have been 10 then, 11 maybe.

We had five leagues. 22,000 acres. 33 square miles. Cummings Hacienda, everyone called it. All of an empire, we thought. All the lumber that went into building up San Felipe, all that wood come from our sawmill. John said, we Cummings' built that town.

We had cattle. Thousand head maybe. Slaves. Three dozen maybe. And when you figure they was going $300 to $600 to $900 a head, a chattel I mean, reckon we was rich. Walkin' in tall cotton.

I do now remember that date. It was fate. Can't forget it. Don't want to. September 2, 1833. That night, it was stormin' out. Thunder, lightning, wind gone all slaunchways. Real cattywampus hummer. Whomperjawed sidewangler, you know. What they used to call a gullywasher. So it's right in the middle of this here frog-strangler that the door to our inn—we'd opened it up only that February out off the east bank of the creek half-a-dozen miles north of San Felipe—the door swings open and sloshing on through wide shouldered comes this figure at once bone-soaked and looking more lost than Adam.

But I could tell straight off he was a gentleman. Trigged out that way with them knee-high shining shop-mades and wide-awning white hat and blue shawl-cape. Toffed up, you know. Rag proper. Kind of man pays as much mind to his wardrobe as his women and not on *account* of his women neither. Straightaway I thought him a cavalier. Cavalier and swashbuckler. Straight off.

Something in his carriage. Forward, but without the swagger, like he owned it, ground he walked on. Whaddya call—self-assured, self-possessed, serious-minded. So it was sort of comical, man like that, so sober-sided, it was an amusement, a man like that looking so sorry and wore out and wrung wet, rain slicking off him in gantlets, just a-flowing off his hat brim, flouncing off in flumes.

Tells us he's got all turned around out there and needs to put up 'til morning. He looked turned around all right, turned around and wet. Angry too. All bowed up, you know. Or not angry, but peeved, put out—with himself, you know—on account of the embarrassment of it. Looking foolish enough to 'a gone and got all caught out that way.

So right there was the first time we landed eyes on each other. Didn't exchange a word. Just laid on looks. Not leers, not oglings, but each glance, each glimpse a character. I do remember that.

Must have been a week or two later he started coming around, catting around, dropping in fair regular-like, two, three times a month. Until with time we got to palavering some, then some more, then confabulating a lot more, and before I know it, he's escorting me to old Ira Lewis's Christmas fandango. Belle of the ball he calls me, and so I am, dancing the night away. Best rugcutter in Texas bar none, clean swan-footed, Will was. Owned two pair of dancing pumps, one black, one red. Two!

And then, after a stretch of sparking, March, early, he asked me please for a lock of my hair, which I don't see the harm, and gave me my first presents—package of cinnamon and this here ivory breast brooch carved up in the figure of a ruby-eyed catamount which he knew by then I was partial to. Prized it then. Prize it still. And in exchange took off my ring, a "cat's eye," and gave him that, which he tried on right there, onto his pinkie finger which it wouldn't, being too big around, so took to wearing it on a knotted whang looped round his neck; periapt.

And then out of the blue, just like that, he was down on a knee asking for my hand.

Well, you could have knocked me over with a featherduster. We'd known each other how long? Five, six months? Didn't feel enough yet. Whirlwind. And then, too, I knew his reputation. Everyone did. His taste for it, you'll pardon the expression. I mean, I knew by then who he was. What's that word? Voluptuary? Which I don't think he was, not all of him, not like Three-legged Willie. A part, maybe. Some part. Small part.

We all knew about Anahuac. Knew too he was an almighty favorite of Mister Austin, enough so he'd just got himself elected secretary of the colony. Knew his law practice over in San Felipe was up and panning out to beat the band. Knew he was propertied, so on. But it was then he let out with the news— he warn't a widower, way he'd let on, but a lawful, spoken-for, married man. And with a child! But that he was divorcing. Had the papers all drawed up, which he showed me.

So that, you can imagine, come as a right shock. Put a fair knot in things, cuz right then, heat of the moment, I was much of a mind to break it off, wait on the legalities. I won't trim. Indeed I did pitch a fit or two, pitched all of a hiss. But by then we was too much each for the other, all of a mash, just both way too plumb sweet. I'd set my cap, lit my candle, and that was that. So the next month, early April, we was engaged, pledged for all time, beatin' hearts betrothed.

When I cipher it up, calculate on it, we had a year-and-a-half of spooning. Such nice times, nice as I ever had. Naughty times too. Being young together, young and loving, in love, doing what young lovers do, a fair lot of ravishing. Reckoned we'd have more, of course, why wouldn't I? All the more in the world, our world, the one we'd build each for the other.

Will was something. A charmer. Chancer. That private privateer's grin of his. And a right good lover. Gentleman lover. Gentle lover with me, always. Why be shy about it?

Too late now to be shy. We was all about a future then, ours, the one folding open like a fan. Everything ahead. Everything possible. Everything promised. All the things a future means, and all it brings.

We listened close, listened patiently to our dreams.

It will surprise some to hear we didn't talk much politics, surprise on account of how he spoke out in public, wrote in the newspapers, walked around armed, so on. But with a thousand dollar bounty on your head, wouldn't you? Those were violent times, or getting to be. It was a violent place, or becoming one. You rode out unarmed at your peril. But then you rode out armed at your peril just the same. He rode out more than most.

Even then I heard some who called him our "Voice." He was just beginning to be called that, Voice of the Revolution. What the Mex called him, of course, was something different. Called him, "The ungrateful, bad citizen, W.B. Travis, who would incite cut-throat revolution against us." All of which would force him into hiding that last summer, whole month of August, '35. Mex never found him, of course. It was Three-legged Willie, found out later, who stashed him, cuz at the time I had no idea, didn't know, he wouldn't say or confide. "For your own good," he said. "Whatever I do, Bec, wherever I wind up, trust me, it's for you and Don Esteban and Texas."

You couldn't ask him to change his ways that way. He was just that man. Standing by, laying off, looking away, keeping still, holding his tongue, letting a thing go, letting it pass, "capitulating to the inevitable," he called it, that wasn't him. Wasn't in him not to do. To *resist*. Some thought it dirty work. He didn't. He called it "my privilege."

"My object, Bec," he told me, "is to behave as a man apart

and re-born and exiled, one entitled to—no, *meriting*—one meriting this country enough to wish to be buried beneath her whenever my time may come, and, afterwards, permit the land to trample my body to mingle as one. I shall never leave this country or look back upon her with nostalgia. I intend to lend more than just a simple hand. It isn't about saving one's own skin. It is about staking one's claim. Staking one's all. All in, to the quick."

And then that October. Second week as I recollect it. Word come that Mr. Austin was calling for volunteers to run the Mex army out of Bejar! That it was occupying Bejar. Bejar, for pity's sake! 150 miles further out west who the hell knows where? So, of course, no questions asked, no odds calculated, not a thought for himself, anything Don Esteban wants. Will was blind willful loyal to that man, I mean to say above all things on this here good green godly earth.

Last time I saw him—in the flesh I mean, cuz I still keep my memories, still have my dreams—I recollect it being January, that week or two after he won his Colonel's rank. He was up on his big-rumped sorrel mare, Flaca, leaning down for our parting kiss. "We will be married when I return," he said and smiled. Struck me, a sad smile, sad in its bluff, its bravery, and off he rode, not a hand-wave good-bye.

And here's the iron in it for you. When he left that day, he was divorced. We didn't know it then, but it had come through at last. We could've been married.

Ain't that just like life? Ain't life just like that?

Looking back, maybe it's best the way it went. I wouldn't have minded, though. Being Mrs. William Barret Travis. I would've been proud, proper proud, wearing his name.

There was a last letter.

The letter from that Alamo didn't reach me until he and the rest was gone, all of 'em *all* gone, not that I knew it at the time. I've lost it long since, but do rightly recollect some three things of it. One was the sweet line, "I shall never be so happy as when I am shed of this wretched place and in your arms again." A second was a piece of flattery pertaining to the nature of my "wiles," the language of which I shan't repeat here. And the third was how he intended to surrender the Alamo if reinforcements did not arrive in the next day or two, along with the promise that he'd be right along home directly soon after.

I never did go there, you know. Never did visit and never will. Couldn't. Can't. Not that place. Its burning ground. Too afraid. Too scared. To hear those dead a-cryin'. Them rough gods a-ridin'. Will's own lamentations. Or worse, his silence.

Don't know what else to say about him. He was this, he was that, some other. I know there were those thought less than kindly of him. Politicians, mainly. That Houston lot. Same ones'll tell you now they was his best friends.

Truth is, he could be a handful. Stand-offish, sure, I saw that, time to time. Fast to rankle, hackle up, too quick-tongued maybe. Tart. Overproud. Meek, mild and malleable, he surely was not. But then, every man, even the best, especially the best, has his shortcomings. His warn't nothing I could not abide.

He was attentive. He paid attention. Catered. Cared. Doted even. Made me feel alive. More alive. Even now, despite the wounding. That there's a rare and precious quality in a person, don't you think? And, you know, we never understand, not really, how deeply we love someone until the moment they are taken from us. We may think we know, but we don't. Because we can't. It is only in their absence that we begin to appreciate the force and fullness of their presence.

The problem with death—well, there's a passel of problems with death, ain't there?—but one of them, one of the hard ones, the one that won't go away, is, when it comes, it stays.

You'd think after all this time, I'd've got over it. Him. Lord knows I've tried, that I keep trying. But you can't clean a person out of you with a wish, and forgetting don't come easy.

I still miss him. I surely sorely do.

What I'd like to know is whether we fall in love simply to distract ourselves. To divert our attention, kill time, keep our minds off the one thing, the only thing that really matters. What I'd like to know is, what is the point of beauty? Why all the fuss and foment and folderol? She who cannot be caught, is she whom forever is sought. She who eludes, is she whom is pursued. She who cannot be acquired, is she whom must be possessed.

Intrigue——Bargain——Management——Success
(Travis Diary, March 12, 1834)

I had, then, been living with myself long enough. Good company, but a man tires of it. Finds himself...dwindling.

Becca was a revelation. As for instance that first time when in the dark my fingertips traced the features of her face; those everted, orchidate lips.

And every time thereafter.

We said so much. Left so much unsaid. Left more unsaid than said. That which we said, sufficed.

I craved her. What else is there to say? The appentence. The ataraxy. No script or choreography, master plan, plot. No thought. Lust lifts love as it will regardless, leavens it lovelier. Sheer.

It quickly became—how could it not?—a matter of arriving at precipices, spanning chasms, piercing walls, crossing borders, closing gaps, occupying thresholds, scaling apexes, sifting details, steadying nerves, violating boundaries, charting menustrations of the moon. A matter of falling into one another (beneath that same moon), heart into heart, soul enfolding soul while tenting, so-called, to the touch. Internal touch.

My sense of her scent was of vanilla and anise, licorice and clove; of her taste, tumeric and tamarind, saffron and sea salt. Cucumber perhaps. Sea cucumber perhaps. Something seaworthy. (Of course, tastes differ). Naptha? No. Verbena water? Perhaps. White tea. White musk tea. Steeped.

It was seven miles overland, my place to hers. Things typically take their course if only they are permitted to do so. If we let them. Life does. Typically, even if we don't.

I see her huddling hunched inside her vicuna poncho puffing periodically upon her kaolin clay pipe, reading my palm, remarking how, "Your life does matter, in the event you were wondering, which, I could not help noticing, you were. Friendly word? Look forward. Leave the looking back to me. You're only as good as you last."

Mysterious, such scrying. To me at least. Witchy woman. But then, as she was wont to suggest, there are occasions when we wonder whether we can or do or ought believe what we believe, apprehend what we believe we apprehend, that impel us to question the nature of that which remains *un*seen, imperceptible beneath, beyond, within.

Even now I am at a loss to explain, despite my suspicion at the time, how one thing inevitably leads co-extensively far and further away from another.

She, for her part, was stricken, haunted by the unsettling implications of a presentiment describing an event or episode entailing watchfires extinguished along the watchtowers, dumped in a pit, stacked on a pyre, buried borne upon billowing winds before brooding unbidden upon the ruins wrought by a tyranny pledged to purge and pogrom.

Ashes to that which is less than ashes.

I might have listened, better. Better, had I listened.

She knew. Claimed to know: "The least is yet to come. Dying, going to heaven, discovering you don't much like it there as much as you thought you might, or, conceivably, at all. A blessing of sorts. Here today, gone later today. Your life is in your hands. Inscribed there, scripted, pre-written. *Amor fati.* You needn't hold it near.

"The dead will be carried ungently, their load pitched and tossed, their mass grave excavated of communal fires. Wait your turn. Sit tight. Establish a fix upon the specifics. First principles. Articles of faith. Emblazon boundaries. Prioritize. Eschew deceit. Know when never to quit. Only the tough last longest.

"There conceivably will be any number of sole survivors. A conspiracy of one or less.

"Life is not personal, but, of course, neither is it impersonal. Say what you will, there *are* moments. A matter of rhizomes. Splice and suture, suture and splice. So it seams. Of sift and sieve. Panned gold. Be patient. All that glitters is seldom clear. It blinds.

"You share very little in common with yourself, don't you?"

All very well, but as I say, I was more wont to be occupied seeking her face, the face *behind* the face, hidden face, naked face, <u>original</u> face, the one before we were born, before the world was made, before it presumed. (Masks have their place, but recognition need not follow. Inscrutability, even opacity inevitably reveal more than can their counterparts. Clarity is complex. It clarifies less often than it complicates.)

All the middles of the night that I awoke unquenched to forage, ravish, to rampage her face with mine eyes—her several smiles as she slept—savor it in a single, endless, unmediated swallow. Better moments I had never known, or would.

She said, continuing, that, "There exists little choice in life but to live it. As its hand may be dealt. Proceed accordingly. So much is pure fiction. The cards do not care. This is nothing new. There can be nothing new between a man and a woman. No one, not a soul, ever taught anyone anything, not a single simple thing about love. There is much to be said for *el estilo mexicano.* I forget just what."

I was drawn to her flaws no less than her flavors. What others doubtless would have called flaws.

She knew, knew that I knew, that her voice was not unpleasant, if too diapason, often inaudible, curiously soft, mallow-soft. My habit was to foot-tap to her fricatives or hum in consecution, as less often to her sweetbriar triphthongs, her plosives scarce less.

Her feet were outsized, especially for one as lightfooted as she.

Neither jug nor ladle-eared, beetled of brow or lanterned of lithic jaw.

Attractive of thickset thigh, toned of well-defined bum, the slots between her toes, I recall very well, being redolent of shaved ginger and fresh mint muddled and mulled.

A blaze of birthmark the color of iodine saddled her nose. I was now and then tempted to mount it, gallop it high and homeward.

Her yawns, thanks be, seldom emerged as groans; her laughter seesawed delightfully, as if in solar/lunar balance.

Intimacy. My god! What a word, last word! What a *con*cept! The mossy precincts, the mangrove swamps, the quayside quim, the shoal-less ciliated fund and foliated fetch, I mean vetch of all *that* lot—creased, greased, gashed and groomed. The gush from its groove, V'd there. Bah!

"Passions are not cling peaches, kid." She was decidedly earnest upon the subject. "You cannot can or jar them, preserve, store, stock them shadowed on a shelf hid aslant the sun, any more than you can waltz with the rainfall or ride high the west wind. For they will find a way. Some entangling way. Bank on it."

We would ride out on dewlapped mornings against the high winds, into the tall grass, switch and grama, fast and hooving faster, adept with speed, aiming to outrace the other, lose ourselves amidst the antelope, the pronghorns whinging up over the river, crossing the Brazos. We might fish some, though I despise fishing. Strip down, peel off, she undoing her torsade, swim naked in dips and plunges, she eeling over me, under, over, swing of hair, sweep of water, laughter like small arms fire.

At such times, sacred times, delirious times, deliriously sacred times, an oozing would pleat over us as a honey fresh from its combs. Of a sudden, then, nothing could have been more natural than that our minds leave in advance, confident that we would, as we never failed to do, meet up with them later, having followed lockstepped, bereft of right axis. Left disarrayed, yes. Disarranged, yes. Left winded, but lighter. Lightened.

"Ah, so *this* is intimacy." I thought then. "This. Here. Now." Remember thinking then, will always remember thinking: "Use my flesh as parchment. Draw your dreams in skin."

She knew—how, I never knew, was never to know—a number of wiles (so-called). These beguilingly occultish maneuvers that, if daunting, were no less besotting. How limber she was! How lubricious! From co-mingled fluids to trans-mingled foams, The Impartress of Pleasure, full-throated if no less full-blown.

Now, one is as accountable for one's own fancies and foibles as in like measure one's fallacies, no? But we are owed nothing, entitled to nothing by right of birth or sweat of brow, though it redoundeth naught to say so, hand to heart or hellbound.

"When are you happiest?" She was interested in knowing. "What makes you happiest?"

Wished, then, that I could have said. Wish I knew even now. "Autumn maybe. Days of the leaves. The high heatherlight, harvest light fallen slant across knap and thatch. Listening to the leaves change their several scents. Quince, or char. Feeling one with, within the parade of death color. The dismantling and disassemblage as orange through the gray, dissolving. The pull of that pall, its pallor decomposing to sap. Autumn is all I ever could ask.

"There also is something in the hoot of the owl that I find deeply, disconcertedly comforting. A connection at a middling distance. But why? My thoughts often resonate with the music woven of the penny whistle. That's some consolation, I'd like to say.

"I don't know. I don't. The way night caves in? Something in the stars? To wish upon or steer by? There rather than here. And in the midst of it, the self-interrogation. In those moments when I *am* self-interrogating. The contunded immanence of it all, the contused immutability. It is too much. I am too much. Too *fuerte*. Take from me what you will. Or can. Hurry, I need you to. I'm yours."

"Then I will help you."

"Please, do. Please help me. Cathect me. Help me stand up on my own." Or, I did not say, I shall fall apart, go to pieces, smithereen amidst this chaos, this Tejas, knowing it will never be the same. Ever again.

O, those were the days. Those were a sheer tumble-down of trans-celestial hours as real as any fantasia or phantasmagoria you might have a hankering or the capacity to right conjure.

Setting the world afire.
Setting his soul afire.
Setting fire to the dark soul of his world.
Firing his soul through the darkness of the world.

His energy a leap at the needle's eye, intact, aflame, out the other side. *Smoking.*

His charred Valhalla soul.

Travis Diary, Nov. 10, 1834:

What is this word *duende* that I overhear certain of the Mexicans using on occasion? I've often asked, but can grasp no answer that makes sense to me. They speak of *alma cómo la fuerza*, soul as force. What does that mean? They refer to *un grito de dolores de salvaje maravilla*, a cry of pain of wild wonder. I fail to make heads or tails. But it intrigues me. Clearly, it must be some kind of quality, human quality, or perhaps a condition of some sort, existential condition. I do not know. I believe the Mexicans have a different way of speaking of such things, a way of endowing death with life, even vitality. They seem to feel life is more complete, *más todo*, in partnership with death, as if death is its missing companion piece. I have heard them say that death looks forward to life. Curious. *Dar a los muertos un poco de vida*, they say—give the dead a little life. Certainly they seem at home with it, at their ease, almost friendly, certainly familiar. They pray to skulls here, those of their loved ones. They dance with skeletons, *osamentas*. They prepare *ofrendas*, offerings of food and drink for what they believe are the dead's living souls. They designate a day, *el día los muertos, jornada del muerto*, to celebrate them. All of this can only strike one as macabre, and yet they seem quite content, even joyous about benefiting by this relationship. I once asked one of our Mexicans here, one of our "old ones," an elder, whether he wasn't afraid of death. No, he replied evenly, *no hay miedo, porque la vida nos has curado de miedo*—there is no fear because life has cured us of fear. There is only *duende*, he said. *Duende, solamente.* That mysterious word again. Not that every last thing is or must be possessed of a literal meaning. Some few things, perhaps many things are possessed of no meaning at all, at least none that is discernible, none that parses, and, for that, perhaps, are in their being, their presence, more profound. That which is too clear, too precise, too concrete, after all, is, as a rule, difficult to understand. Don Esteban dismisses it as, "so much Mexican metaphysics," but I believe there may be more to it than that. I do not know, but I believe that I would like to.

SANTA ANNA

When Antonio de Padua María Severino López de Santa Anna y Pérez de Lebron—also known as he much preferred to be known, demanded to be known, as, "The Napoleon of the West" or, alternatively, The Imposer of Unforeseen Destinies—when S.A. ascended to the presidency of Mexico as a member of his country's Liberal Party, we reckoned that matters were about to inflect in our favor at last: that the Anti-immigration Law that Don Esteban had lobbied against so long and so diligently would be summarily repealed; that the many military garrisons throughout the territory would be dismantled; that the astronomical tariffs on imported goods from the States would be lowered if not eliminated; and that laws against the formation of local militias and ownership of chattel would be relaxed.

Perhaps, we dared pray, Texas even would be granted some form of independence.

It was this last matter on behalf of which Stephen Austin intended to lobby when he undertook to travel the 1,000 miles south, our own newly-drafted Texas state constitution in hand, to meet with the new president, our putative champion, in Mexico City late that fall. Instead, in the wake of their discussions, as we in time received reports from that place, he found himself by S.A.'s explicit order, under arrest, clamped in irons and dungeoned in solitary confinement as a political prisoner. With no specific criminal charge brought—there was talk of a trumped up "sedition" case, but no formal papers ever were filed—he remained unindicted throughout the course of his 14-month *calabozo*-ing. We were incredulous.

Locking up Stephen Austin was, of course, an outrage. It outraged everyone, nor was that outrage confined merely to the colony. In our official capacities as colonial administrators, Willie and myself immediately wrote and published in the local press a series of outraged broadsides which we sent on to Santa

Anna, in outrage, demanding Don Esteban's release. Meanwhile, there was outraged talk of escape plans and jailbreaks and night raids, all of which remained precisely that—talk. Outraged talk.

What was not talk, outraged or otherways, was what Santa Anna presumed to do next. Namely, in a power grab so nakedly audacious that it would have stunned Machiavelli, he dissolved the Mexican National Congress, dissolved each of the local state legislatures and their state militias, abolished the Federal Constitution, declared himself Supreme Dictator—Military Despot was nearer the truth—garrisoned thousands of Mexican soldiers throughout Texas, and in the presence of the U.S. Consul threatened to, "march on the Capital and lay Washington City in ashes," should the United States dare intervene.

Those possessed of the temerity to oppose him, he and his army summarily crushed, as he directly did the recalcitrant state of Zacatecas during a two day spree of rape and ransack that resulted not only in the massacre of that state's militia, but the mass murder of 2,000 of its citizens. Message sent, message received. The brute and brutal days had come again.

Government-sanctioned massacre as a calculated extension of his political will, was, as we were to learn soon enough, something that Santa Anna excelled at. It was as if, in order to survive, to feel more alive, as alive as possible in himself, he needed to inspire fear in others. This despot and tyrant who, because he feared the worst in everyone else, felt the need to engage in behaviors designed to make others fear the worst in him. Needed, that is, to embrace cruelty and spread terror and exact revenge as a way of preventing himself from being consumed by his own inadequacies. To release and *discharge* the rage with which he daily lived, by visiting it upon others, regardless of their guilt or innocence.

Nor, by the way, is *all* of this theorem.

Not that any of us felt anything but sheer loathing for the man, but in my estimation, Señor Santana was one pitifully sad case. Not that that sadness was unmerited, for he damn well had earned it, and a damnsight more, owing to his unremitting intrigues and duplicitous subterfuges, intrigues and subterfuges that would see him, whether through rigged elections, backroom machinations, mob rule or military coup, ascend to and lose the Mexican presidency—and along the way a left leg, to grapeshot—eleven times over 27 years. Until, at last, he had succeeded in so alienating his people, a people so wearied of his public posturing, narcissistic ambition and amoral opportunism, ill-advised and incompetent military adventuring and meddlesome treachery—not to mention his profligate gambling, indiscriminate whoring (he sired well over a half-dozen bastard children) and predatory plundering of the public purse—that, the government having seized his assets and confiscated his properties (he owned, by then, a dozen haciendas and 10,000s of square miles of land) he was left little choice but "perpetual exile."

And so the two decades of nomadic banishment began: first to Cuba, then Jamaica, then Colombia, then St. Thomas, then the Dominican, finally to the Bahamas, until, 80 years old, crippled, blind and destitute, he was permitted to return to the country he so often had both spectacularly failed and unconscionably abused that he might die alone and despised, though not forgotten utterly.

But all that was still ahead, far, far in the future. For the present, as if his maltreatment of Austin was not enough, as it so clearly was not, then did this blennorhagic so-called Napoleon order his War Department, specifically his fanatically anti-American Minister of War, José María Tornel, to issue "Circular Number Five," *Octavilla Numero Cinco*, more infamously known as The Tornel Decree, upon the publication of which he, S.A., remarked:

> With this decree we hereby put the American pirates, cabalists, and conspirators on notice that no longer shall we abide their ingratitude towards and perfidious abuse

of the Mexican people whose natural disposition is to be humane and compassionate in all things. Forgetting what they owe the supreme government of this nation which admitted them to its nurturing bosom, gave them fertile lands to cultivate and allowed them all the means to live in comfort and abundance, they nonetheless have risen against that same government for the criminal purpose of dismembering the territory of this Republic. In consequence their day is now done. They ought not have been permitted to settle here in the first instance. If they are wise they will heed the words of this decree and leave of their own accord before they are compelled to leave by other less peaceful means.

The Decree

MEXICO CITY
War and Navy Department

Circular No. 5:

The government has received information that in the United States of North America meetings are being called for the avowed purpose of getting up and fitting out expeditions against the Republic of Mexico in order to send assistance to the rebels, foster the civil war, and inflict upon our country all the calamities by which it is followed.

In the United States of North America, our ancient ally, these expeditions have been furnished with every kind of ammunition, by means of which the revolted colonies of Tejas are enabled to resist and fight the nation from which they received but immense benefits. The government is also positively informed that these acts, condemned by the wisdom of the laws of the United States, are also reported by the general government with which the best intelligence and greatest harmony still prevail.

However, as these adventurers and speculators have succeeded in escaping the penalties inflicted by the laws of their own country, it becomes necessary to adopt measures for their punishment, and so the President, anxious to repress these aggressions which constitute not only an offense to the sovereignty of the Mexican nation, but also to evident violation of international laws as they are generally adopted, has ordered the following decrees to be enforced.

1. Foreigners landing on the coast of the republic or invading its territory by land, armed with the intention of attacking our country, will be deemed pirates and dealt with as such.

2. All foreigners who will import either by sea or land, in the places occupied by the rebels, either arms or ammunition of any kind for the use of them, will be deemed pirates and punished as such.

3. The rebels themselves, and their leaders, one Travis high among them, being not only traitors, but citizens of no nation presently at war with the republic, and fighting under no recognized flag, are hereby deemed de facto pirates who have forfeited all legal standing and entitlement to judicial consideration, and will be dealt with summarily as such, the government of the republic arrogating to itself the right to execute them by hanging or firing squad.

—Jose Maria Tornel, *Secretaria de Guerra y Marina*

And then there was this addendum, signed by Santa Anna himself: "Immediately and without excuse, we must proceed to the apprehension of the ungrateful and bad citizen Barret Travis, fugitive head of the Revolutionary Party, and cause him to be placed at the disposal of the principal Commandant of the State in order that he may be tried and punished as he is an injury to the inhabitants of Tejas and it is a shame that they should in cold blood be tolerating his excuses when he should have been punished long since."

Up Country

Word of the order for my apprehension and arrest issued out of Matamoros reached San Felipe, 350 miles north, with just time enough for Willie and myself to saddle up and light out. Get the hell hellbent gone and away. Until further notice we were hunted men. Manhunted men. Should our pursuers, those *Federales*, have caught up to us, succeeded in hunting us down, we knew we were dead men.

Losing ourselves "Up Colony," we spent the month of August on the run, incommunicado, lying low, ghosts gone to ground. Wild country up there, bush country, no man's land, all-but-Indian country, that of the Comanche, Caddo, Witchita, Waco. We pushed north. Pillar to post, hand to mouth, catch as catch can, but always north. Further north, seldom lingering more than a day or two in any one place.

Camp, break camp, decamp. Pick up, pack up, vamoose, become vapor. Pushpushpush. Skirted *Comancheria* itself, its southeast edge. All of which was terra incognita to me, though Willie claimed to know it, "better'n I know my own handyanked pecker."

Later I listed, or mapped actually, mapped as much as I could piece together the where and with whom we had put up:

Gay Hill, 50 miles up the Brazos, a few uneventful days with Horatio Chriesman, Don Esteban's Chief of Surveyors, his place on La Bahia Trace. (Willie, it quickly became apparent, knew *every*one. Or, where he did not, knew someone who did.)

Fanthrop, 40 miles west, with a Cornish couple as brave as they were graciously gregarious, Postmaster Henry and Rachel Fanthorp, corncrib out back of their newly-built dogtrot cabin.

Tenoxtitlan, backtracking east, another 50 miles north, stowed-away courtesy of Princeton Theological Seminary-educated Reverend Peter Fullinwider and his bride, Balinda, faithful Presbyterians both. (They raised orchards. Invited us to load up on unripened apples, peaches, pears, persimmons, pawpaws, plums. We frighted off bears for mul and huckle berries.)

Sarahville, technically Sarahville de Viesca, another 75 miles north, stashed loftside above the stables of Arabian horsebreeder Clack Robertson, his place at the Falls of the Brazos.

Parker, another 30 miles north and east, Elder John and Duty "Granny" Parker's "Indian-proof fort" at the disconsolate, desolate headwaters of the Navasota.

As such potentially sidewise experiences go, ours, in the end, thank god, largely was bereft of high drama save for that which unfolded night after night across the most vivid, what I can only describe as graphically paganistic dream sequence of my life.

Not that looking over one's shoulder 24 hours a day, day after Moruga-hot day, hardset on outdodging death, or sleeping most of a week raw-sore in the saddle, or hip-slung highmost in trees, or basted in mud to one's knees beneath reeds and branches and weeds brined to the bone burnt black to a scab clawed bloody by sawbriar and devil's hair, or being sucked on by leeches and eaten half-alive by bat-sized skeeters, or driven mostways mad by gadflies, or waking to a nest of scorpions in one's boot or chiggers at one's crotch or up one's arse, is half-fun, but we sidestepped death by water moc or rattler or timber wolf, the Comanch did not lift our skullcaps, we saw neither hide nor hearsay of the Mex, and Willie's friends, our fellow Texians, never refused us a gnaw or a brace or a bivouac or the send-off of a good Protestant prayer as the occasion may have engendered it or we solicited of them much the same.

With news up from home that "the coast's all clear," we were back in San Felipe by the end of the month to huzzahs, hugs and fandangos all around where, cheered on to it by the our local citizenry, I publicly avowed, that, "If they want me now, they know where to find me. I'm not going anywhere. No more running. No more hiding. If they want me now, here I am. If they want me now, come and get me. If they want me now, let them try."

Travis Diary, Oct. 4, 1835:

War at last! Word arrives of an affray gone off yesterday at Zeke Williams's Gonzales farm and our intent, once our numbers are sufficient, to advance upon *Bejar* and oust the Mexican garrison there under the command of Santana's brother-in-law, Cos. This is it. It has come. S.A.'s campaign to disarm us, castrate, cut off our *cojones*, geld us bloody, to leave us defenseless without the means or wherewithal to resist. Details trickle in from Gonzales of 100 Mex dragoons sent to fetch off one of our home-made cannon and our refusal at gunpoint to permit it. *Come and Take It!* A skirmish leaving two Mex dead, not a one of ours. They are routed, in retreat. Hurrah boys! Huzzahs Clint Neill! Kudos Jimmy Fannin! "We flogged them like hell!" Our Lex & Concord Moment, and me, here, flat on my back with this fucking fucking flu! "Pioneering is not feeling well," wrote Anne Bradstreet. And frontiering, dear poetess, is delirium. Still, damn! How I hate missing history.

Travis Diary, Nov. 28, 1835:

Once more I find myself upon my return to San Felipe the abashed beneficiary of a most flattering welcome by the good citizens here for doing no more than duty required in leading the late raid that won for our side without loss of a single man some 300 of the enemy's mounts in the vicinity of the San Miguel Creek 60 miles southward of *Bejar*. Gratified as I am by the published commendation affirming my "personal worth, distinguished service and quiet valor" in this affair, my concern at present is for those hundreds of my countrymen who have chosen to remain behind to sustain what is now well in excess of our month-long investment of that *Bejar* place. Pray God that they may succeed in securing their object with but a minimum of blood shed or life lost.

Travis Diary, Dec. 12, 1835:

Cos has surrendered! We have taken *Bejar* at last, and, if reports are to be believed, with but four dead and two dozen wounded! Surely this is the best of Christmas miracles. This night, jubilation and jamboree. This night, for Rebecca.

Travis Diary, Dec. 16, 1835:

As the new year approaches, no further word about *duende*. No *más palabras*. Frustrating, *este rompecabézas*. I continue to inquire, probe, make of myself a damn nuisance. But no. *Nada*. For now, no better understanding, firmer grasp. And yet, I am persuaded more now than ever that unless and until I can excavate this word, penetrate fully, wholly, its many levels, step through its bottom to lift it topside, evacuate this word as if it were a part of my own body, unless and until that moment of....disinterment, my inexplicable love for this place, this Tejas, must, at least in part, *una parte más importante*, remain stillborn. There is a dark secret here, I am convinced of it. But am I close to unlocking it? Any closer than I have ever been? To intuiting the music of its many meanings? No. I suspect not. I suspect that I am not close. I am not close at all.

Chaz

I wanted my son. It had been long enough. More than four years. I was intent now upon insisting that I should have my son. Be granted sole custody of my son. If Rosanna wanted her freedom, as she had some months past written to me, if she wished to be free to marry this Sam Cloud person back in Alabama, then I wanted my son. She could keep her daughter, who for all I knew was not my daughter. I wanted and would have my son.

I did not want my flesh and blood reared by a man who was not his flesh and blood. I did not want my son calling another man, a different man, a man other than myself, father. Nor did I want his mother to have him. I wanted to deprive her of having him.

Because, frankly, I was frightened. Lately, I was having dreams of the death of my son. I dreamt nightly of the death of my son. Run over by a wagon, bucked off a horse, trampled by beeves, bitten by a rabid dog, struck by lightning, burned up in a fire, drowned in a river, pitched out of a tree, fallen down a snakepit, swarmed by yellowjackets, lost in a swamp, eaten by wild beasts, felled by pox and fever. The death scenarios were infinite.

I wanted, now, to keep him near me. I needed to. To keep him safe. My own peace of mind.

She could have her daughter. I wanted my son.

I was not sentimental about it, but I cared about caring for him. Felt responsible. And, yes, did not want him to grow up without me. Knowing me. At least a little. And that I loved him. In my way.

Insofar as possible, I intended to make up for lost time, the absent years.

I knew we are strangers. I knew that well enough.

With a minimum of fuss, surprisingly, little but some meager nominal resistance from his mother, Chazzie joined me that spring. (Why did she not fight me on this? Had she ceased to hate me? I hoped not. She should hate me. It did her no credit not to hate me. Perhaps she did not love her son.)

Six years old. Or soon to be.

Honestly, though, what did I know of six-year-old boys? Or about fathering one, parenting one? The memory of my own was hardly helpful; no model there. Whether my natural instincts, paternal instincts, parental instincts are the correct ones, or even if I am possessed of them, I could only wonder. I knew only what I recalled from having once been one myself, a six-year-old boy.

I recalled little enough.

Depositing Chaz out of harm's way with my friend David Ayres at his Methodist boarding school up in Montville, I visited him there as I was able, if not as often as I might have preferred. When I did visit, however, I made certain not to arrive empty-handed. I brought him presents. Molasses candy on a cord, a bag of marbles, a pocketknife, an ivory *balero*, an ocarina. Did I expect that such tokens would endear me to him? Was I endeavoring to win his love by buying him off with cheap bribes? Trying to bridge a lifetime's distance with trinkets?

When he told me that he had his heart set on his own pony, I promised him, perhaps later. Then a dog, he said. More possible, I replied. I told him then that when I was his age, I had a pet owl named Oswald. Mister Oz. Ozzie. What I did not tell him was that our family also had dogs, kept dogs, several dozen dogs that his grandpa had bred and rebred and crossbred and inbred, dreaming of producing what he called "the perfect fighting speciman," and which, in the end, predictably enough, produced quite the opposite—a maniacal race of distempered, half-blind, pariah mutants, most of which either died off young of their own grotesque and wayward defects, or had to be put down in the wake of having been gang-mauled by their half-crazed, blood-hungry packmates.

Tousling his slapdash shock of chestnut hair, I instructed him please to stop calling me "Sir," that "Father" would do quite nicely. We arm and thumb wrestled; he won two out of three. We footraced; he beat me by a country mile. Had breath-holding contests; he outlasted me twice over. I taught him how to whistle, shuffle a deck of cards, tie a slipknot, negotiate a handstand, swim the backstroke, play mumblety-peg, count sheep to sleep, how to write his name backwards then hold it to a mirror, cup a hummingbird in his hand. Using blunt-tipped wooden staves, I taught him how to parry and thrust.

I asked him questions about himself, what he liked, what he didn't, if he had any special magical powers, secret abilities or hidden identities, lucky charms or tutelary spirits.

What I did not ask him, made a point of not asking him, was, "Do you miss your mother?"

single extant image of Travis "from life" is a pen-and-ink sketch idly doodled by San Felipe friend and fellow duelist, Wyly Martin, dated December 1835. This being a chest-up "fair likeness" showing a broad-shouldered man in his youthful prime with noticeably receding hairline and jaw-long sidewhiskers framing a face possessed of regular, pleasant enough features, bearing a distant, even dreamy, not entirely distracted gaze above a thin-lipped, bemused half-smile.

The impression is that of a minister's philosophical only son. Philosophical or poetical. Anything but a firebrand spirit embodying the hopes, dreams and aspirations of any damn one, much less all of a frontier.

Or, needless to say, but let us say it anyway, an inspirational leader of men.

Its authenticity remains a matter of dispute, as does its accuracy.

Voices

"He was uncommonly brainful while being noted for neither an abundance of wit nor humor, both of which traits rendered him rather less beloved than he might otherwise have been. For the most part, in the brief time we knew one another, I cannot say that we got on. Still I could not help feeling a certain amount of pity for a man who so hungered to be admired, but, however much he might in certain respects have richly deserved it, had no idea whatever how to go about winning it." (J. Hampton "Hamp" Kuykendall, Apprentice at Law to W.B. Travis, Esq.)

"*Travis tuvo el* **duende** *de diez hombres y el corazón valiente de un león, pero su temperamento poético con demasiada frecuencia nublo su mejor juicio.*" (Travis had the **duende** of ten men and the brave heart of a lion, but his poetical temperament too often clouded his best judgment.) "I believe he wanted better for us. *Mi gente.* My people. He had *el corazón.* The heart. He had *el cerebro.* The brain. He had *los cojones.* The balls. He had *ganas.* The will and desire. When I heard the news of his death, I wept, I drank, I danced." (Juan N. Seguin)

"Brilliant, brave, brash, brusque—in that order. A young man of inestimable even transcendant talents. Had he lived he eventually would have been elected President of Texas, of that there can be little doubt, anymore than that he would have flatly refused the office. He was just that smart. No self-aggrandizing Houston. No swaggering Bowie. He was stalwart. I loved him like a son." (Stephen Fuller Austin)

"Not a man I put much stock in, frankly. Stirred up more trouble than he was worth. Not just an intemperate hothead, but one with a high-and-mighty opinion of himself. Impossible to control, and he desperately required controlling since he was so incapable of controlling himself. Consider the way he died. Wholly unnecessary. A grand waste. All those deaths were." (Sam Houston)

"He treated me mean and shabby. Did me dirt. I don't forgive'm, but I'm right sorry he died. Way he died. Fondle better'n the fuck sort. You know the kind. Talked a better poke 'n' he ever put out. Never did know true bleakness 'til I knowed him." (Rosanna Cato)

"Most-wise, he massa me kindly. No lash or hand laid on. Clad me fine. Kept warm of winters. But ain't yer say. Goes where's yer tol. Even hell. Died a man on them walls. There beside him. Seen it all. Died a man. Gone on home now to Jesus." (Joe, Travis's man-servant)

"That young man was a credit to his race and a boon ornament to his time. White race. Troubled time. I am proud to claim him as a native son of our fair state. His like walks among us too seldom. I might wish we had a hundred more of his kind here. Hell, I wish we had a thousand!" (C.C. Clay, Governor of Alabama)

Houston

Sam Houston, frankly, I did not much care for—and here, at the risk of sounding the backbiter, I should pause briefly to explain why I did not much care for Sam Houston.

I did not much care for Sam Houston, not owing to his being a hopeless sot—the Mexicans not incorrectly call him *El Gran Borracho*, the Big Drunk—or because he was an equally hopeless, self-congratulatory, devious boor and liar who lied even when it was unnecessary to do so, but because he had convinced himself that he and our cause, Don Esteban's cause, the cause of Texas, were one and the same, and that what was good for Sam Houston was good for Texas, and that if certain hard sacrifices, mortal sacrifices on the part of others were required to ensure that Sam Houston succeeded in realizing his private ambitions, which in fact were little more than Andrew Jackson's private ambitions—namely, to annex Texas to the United States and anoint Sam Houston its first headman—then those sacrifices, human sacrifices, were acceptable ones.

If the world needed to die that Sam Houston might live, live and ascend—*soar*—then the world needed to die, no apologies extended. Everything, everyone else was expendable.

Sam Houston was a devourer of the flesh of others that he might give his own life a run for its money. Money and fame and power.

I might wish that this was hyperbole. It is not hyperbole.

Houston, who had on more than one occasion dismissed Austin as "a viper without fangs"—though if Austin was a viper, then might I suggest that Houston was a vulture, six feet two inches of vulture—Houston was a man who was all for Houston. While Austin, to draw the required distinction, was a man who was all for Texas.

Now, whether Austin loved Texas as much as Houston loved Houston, I should hesitate to venture, but certainly the latter was not the man who over the past 15 years—15!—had in the name of defending the lives and livelihoods of his friends and neighbors suffered personal insult, physical breakage, material impoverishment and 14 months confined to a Mexican dungeon. Indeed, at the behest of Jackson, Houston had been in Texas scarcely three.

This, in part, was why I did not much care for Sam Houston, a feeling, so my impression, that was nothing if not mutual. Despite his favorite son status with Washington D.C. as Andrew Jackson's intimate and political protege, despite his access to those corridors of power, despite in a word, his *clout*, I did not trust him.

Having politicked his way to being appointed Major-General and Commander-in-Chief of the so-called Federal Regular Army of Texas—the man was a genius politicker, no eyeblink was uncalculated—it was on Christmas Day 1835 that Houston commissioned me his Lieutenant Colonel Commanding of Cavalry, tasking me to raise a troop of 400 men-of-horse, after which I was to proceed the 150 miles west to San Antonio de Bejar, the largest town in Texas (pop. 2,507), to join with the men garrisoning an old Spanish mission there called, so I was told, the Alamo, then under the command of our Colonel of Artillery, Clint Neill.

In doing so, Houston made it plain to me that he in fact had little use for cavalry, that our horsemen could not hope to equal the Mexican's own, that he was strictly an infantry and artillery man. What he made no less plain was that he was convinced that *Bejar* was of little or no real strategic consequence, being a too-isolated outpost that, should it come to it, would be better abandoned and demolished than defended. Ergo, his hollow gesture of a gratuitous commission and superfluous deployment.

He wished me exiled. Or worse.

While it may indeed be the case that humanity adores only those who cause it to perish, adoring of Sam Houston I decidedly was not.

And so, set up to fail, I failed. As Houston knew full well that I must. My recruitment efforts met with abject, humiliating failure. Having succeeded in enlisting precisely 26 men, what choice did I have? I tendered my resignation. Which, Houston, naturally, immediately refused, ordering me instead to proceed with my 26-man "legion," as he sarcastically referred to it, to *Bejar*.

Naturally, I did not want to go. I decided not to go. No, I told myself, I will not go, but first, I will consult Don Esteban, whose affection for Houston all but rivals my own.

When I told Austin that I had decided not to go, that I would not go, he told me, I must say much to my dismay, that I must go, that I had "no conceivable choice" but to go. He appealed to my vanity. And ambition.

"Texas needs you now, Buck," he said in a voice hair-lined with cracks. "This has nothing to do with Houston. The man be a scoundrel, but he is our scoundrel, and if, as General of our army, it is his considered determination that you are needed in *Bejar*, then as both the patriot I know you to be, as well as the soldier I know you are capable of being, it is your duty to go there."

"With respect," I replied, "I shall go on, sir, as it pleases you to counsel. I shall do my duty, forlorn as it is, but the patriotism of a few, while it may do much, cannot do enough. It cannot perform miracles, much less that which is required. And we both know what is required.

"Money. We must raise money, or Texas is lost. In this, I have strained every nerve, exhausted my personal credit twice over, have slept neither day nor night, and yet, despite all this… exertion, the people remain cold and indifferent.

"Where, sir, the fervor? Where, pray tell, the numbers? Numbers in *sufficient* number. Twenty-six, might I be permitted to remind you. The number sickens me. I have succeeded in enlisting but 26! Patriotism is easy, too easy while the sun yet brightly shines."

Now, by the time he returned to Texas after being released from his imprisonment in Mexico City in late '35, Stephen Fuller Austin, while a much-reduced and broken man both in heart and health, also was a much radicalized one, something I apprehended when shortly after his return to San Felipe he had confided to me that, "A year spent detained, Buck, *un rehen*, a hostage, rotting in a Mexican prison at the pleasure of the self-appointed powers that be, deprived of all access to legal representation, denied due process, that sort of experience you may believe can materially alter one's outlook.

"I truly did believe in her once you know, *mi Madre México*. But now? Now must come the final break. Now must war to the hilt and the hub. We must only *Americanize* Texas, Buck. Every other avenue, every conceivable remedy has been utterly exhausted. I will wear myself out by inches before I will submit to Santa Anna."

Poor Don Esteban. He had yet to regain his pallor. His flesh was crepe, his hair tinseled with snow. His teeth, those remaining, were yellowed and browned. His hands visibly trembled. He walked with a stoop; his gait was unsteady. He no longer could mount a horse without assistance.

So much breakage suffered. So much damage done. So much sacrifice made. Too much. He had given too much. Given all. He appeared petrified, some fossilized relic of archaeology. Forty-two years old. He looked 60.

"Go on and do your duty, Buck," he admonished. "Despite all, the paltry number, which I agree is most inauspicious, do your duty, and in the end you will not only have performed a critical public service for our cause in its hour of greatest moment, it will, trust me, redound to your private benefit to have done so. It will, son, save your soul."

I ate crow then, ate several servings of humble pie, swallowed hard, wished Don Esteban godspeed, saddled up, fetched along my slave-boy Joe—where I was bound, I might well, I anticipated, have dire need of a slave-boy—and headed out.

I headed for the Alamo.

"*Giddap!*"

On my way out of San Felipe, I stopped to file a certain legal document with Three-legged Willie. This gesture of prudence. I had a hunch:

I, William Barret Travis, of the town of San Felipe in Austin Colony, State of Texas, & by the law of colonization an adopted citizen of same, who by permission of divine providence now enjoy good health with a sound & disposing mind, believing in the doctrines of Christianity & taking into consideration THE UNCERTAINTY OF LIFE, knowing it is appointed FOR ALL MEN TO DIE & in order that the mind shall at that time BE RELEASED from the care of all temporal concerns, have thought proper to make & publish this act as my Last Will & Testament:

Everything, all of it, only, to my child,
Charles Edward Travis,
and nothing, nothing at all, to everyone else.

"Giddap!"

On January 25th, 1836, Generalissimo Antonio de Padua María Severino López de Santa Anna y Pérez de Lebron addressed the 6,019 assembled troops of his Expeditionary Army of the Republic of Mexico gathered for grand review at Saltillo, the capital city of the state of Coahuila, some 325 miles southwest of San Antonio de Bejar.

Comrades in arms:

Our most sacred duties have brought us to these uninhabited lands and demand our engaging in combat against a rabble of wretched adventurers to whom our authorities have unwisely given benefits that even our Mexican citizens do not enjoy, and who have taken possession of this vast and fertile area, convinced that our own unfortunate internal divisions have rendered us incapable of defending our own soil.

Wretches! Soon they will become aware of their own folly.

Soldiers:

We will march as long as the interests of the nation that we serve demand. The claimants to the acres of Texas land will soon know to their sorrow that their reinforcements from New Orleans, Mobile, Boston, New York, and other points north, whence they should never have come, are insignificant, and that Mexicans, generous by nature, will not leave unpunished affronts resulting in injury or discredit to their country, regardless of who the aggressors may be.

My friends:

Lest you forget, they are nothing but, *una chusma de adventureros desgaciados, bandidos, y asesinos a la que nuestro país tiene desde hace demasiado tiempo imprudentemente concedido el estatuto y los beneficiosa favor inmerecido.* A rabble of wretched adventurers, bandits, and murderers to whom our country has for far too long unwisely granted favored status and unmerited benefits. They are pirates, and as such, must be expelled to their last extremity regardless of whether they have families or not, and all their dwellings need to disappear to the last *jacale* lest they entertain the hope of ever returning to them for shelter.

My loyal brothers:

Be assured that should evidence be discovered that the government of the North American states is materially supporting the rebellion in Texas, I will continue the march of this army to Washington City and raise upon its Capitol the Mexican flag.

He then issued to his generals:

Standing Orders
to the Expeditionary Army of Operations
in *Tejas*

(by authority of His Most Serene and Beneficent Highness, Generalissimo Antonio de Padua María Severino López de Santa Anna de Pérez de Lebron, President and Supreme Leader for Life of Mexico)

Numero Uno: Every Mexican who has fought with the rebels or in any way supported them is to be hanged. No protracted trials. Hang them summarily for treason.

Numero Dos: Every American colonist who has taken arms against us is to be shot. Again, no exceptions, no trials.

Numero Tres: Those who supported the rebels but did not take up arms, are to be expelled forever from Mexican soil.

Numero Cuatro: All American immigrants, regardless of their sympathies, are to be removed at least 100 miles south of the Rio Grande, whether they can bring their household possessions or not.

Numero Cinco: Further immigration from the American states into Tejas or any other part of Mexico is strictly forbidden.

Numero Seis: The people of Tejas are to repay every peso of expense incurred on this expedition to discipline them.

Numero Siete: Any foreigner in Tejas who is arrested while in possession of arms of any kind is to be judged a pirate, treated accordingly and hanged without trial.

Numero Ocho: Most important and to be stressed above all—once the battle has begun, if the enemy has not previously surrendered, <u>no</u> <u>prisoners</u> <u>will</u> <u>be</u> <u>taken</u>. They are to be shot, bayoneted, or lanced upon the field of battle where they are captured.

Travis Diary, Jan. 26, 1836:

There are times when the appeal of an intelligent indifference, a sublime and well-considered disengagement is almost too alluring to resist. Those moments when one wishes only to flee the darkness, the inhumanity, duplicity and corruption, convinced that suffering the world a second longer is inconceivable. And yet, at every turn one finds oneself resisting injustice and tyranny if for no other reason than that some things in this life cannot be permitted to stand. For surely anything that can be taken away will be, inevitably must be if one does not actively resist their being taken. Still, a purpose, a calling, is one thing, but I am not possessed of the fanatic's heart. Indeed, I routinely have sought to dodge embranglement of that sort, the crusader's sort, the zealot's sort. How, then, I find myself so embroiled—it having fallen to me to be the spokesman for such an undertaking—is something I find only confounding. I flabbergast myself, a self that even now persists in believing that those who permit the personal to become political merit whatever form their come-uppance may assume. Perhaps a clue reposes in the distinction to be drawn between Cause and Dream. The moment when one's dream *becomes* one's cause. Perhaps the real peril, the more immediate danger, reposes in our dreams dreaming us. Pursuing us. Consuming us. I never sought the latter. I do not require such meaning. I require only latitude. The time, space and wherewithal to comport the more perfectly with my own nature. Autonomous nature. Sovereign nature. To exercise my *fullest* measure of self-dominion.

Somewhere only god knows where (call it Burnham's Crossing; Colorado River country) lost in the limitless landscape 40 mapless miles west of San Felipe riding west toward *Bejar*, eight of my 26 recruits desert, go more missing than meridians in the night, into the night eight shapeless dwarves disappear dark as water under water absconding with arms and horses.

Goddamn them to no apparent purpose.

Eighteen men now. Down to 18. What am I to do with 18 men? These leftovers. Hold a parade? Form a coven? Mount a search party? Fucking discommodity. *Christ!*

Heading west on some misbegotten dead-end dead-of-winter destination death-mission, each mile feeling more ridiculous than the mile preceding, increasingly immune to deep feeling and cogent thought. Lucidity like scars.

Sure sheer in its shearing the wind here blows and blows. Does not cease blowing. A wolfhound of wind, a *cante jondo* incense-colored and high-howled. Blows and blows chiseling clockwise, counter-clockwise, fraught with punctures pleated with pockets through the whiffles of which a whistling wholesales wounded and raw. Invariably, unvaryingly, **the wrong way.**

Next morning breaking camp at crack of
brought up short by a solitary blue heron
stilt-stiff at my shoulder, silent assassin
bayonet bird lifting riparian through mist
parting sky to wings releasing altitude like silt
sifting soft
one feather at a time.

Travis Diary, Feb. 3, 1836:

Going by first impressions, how be impressed? For fuck sake! This so-called Alamo is a perfect ruin. Its trove of artillery notwithstanding—I am told it is mounted with some 20 cannon—it is little better than a sprawling, bat-infested dumpsite that the recent rains have rendered three acres of squalid swamp sump. Houston may be right after all. Why bother defending such a *cagadero*? Such a latrine. All the more so, as, so I have been informed, it has within the month been systematically stripped of horses, cattle, packmules, oxen, wagons and carts, looted of all clothing and bedding, all medical stores, all comestibles and potables, as well as most of its arms and munitions, the lot fetched off by a rogue element of its own garrison—some 200 armed men—more interested in abandoning their post here to adventure south after such spoils as might present themselves for the plucking than in sitting on their hands inside a stinking slopsink waiting for the enemy to appear. I find it difficult to blame them. At least Bowie has remained behind. He billets in town at his father-in-law's *palacio* and has invited me to visit him there. He has been so good as to arrange for me to take a room on the Main Plaza in town, though from the little I have seen of the latter, it impresses me only slightly more than does this Alamo itself. I confess to doleful feelings, seek solace in Scott's good words: "It is wonderful, what strength of purpose and bold energy of will are aroused by the assurance that we are doing our duty. One hour of life, crowded to the full with glorious action and filled with noble risks, is worth whole years in which men steal through existence without honor." I shall do my duty as it has fallen to me to do it. May God grant me the capacity to see it done. Meanwhile, here I am, down in the dumps, as far and farther than the eye can see.

I entered there, fucking tumbledown papist shambles, horsebacked Main Gate South, high noon higher, 42-degrees, peekaboo sun, prevailing westerlies By some unswerving punctuality of shambolic chance sucked
    —suckered? I already had begun seriously to wonder—

Slanchwise through the four horned walls of the
New   Real   World
        swallowed
                stomached
                        surrounded
                                "Reporting for duty,"
saluting, rueing   the listless day
Scenting sulfur
Chewing windcud
Eating manes of dust (they do not settle, never settle; they *swish*)
    and being eaten in turn

Knew it the moment my boots bit ground
How life is briefer by the moment
How a man tires of being terrified of wishing too much
to love his life
How becoming young once is *just* enough
How history has its own way of catching up with us
                        python, coiling
                            in perpetuity

ven as I found myself prevailed upon by the Alamo's staunch-hearted 45-year-old commander, Clint Neill, Col. James Clinton Neill, the same responsible for touching off the first cannon shot of our revolution at Gonzales some four months past, I was so clutched by feelings of revulsion, inadequacy and dread, that I had all I could do to keep from decorating my boot tops with the acid-churned contents of my stomach. (Coffee *negro*, tortilla, fatback, green chiles, cracked frijoles, *arroz cocido*, god knows what.)

"It is imperative that I leave here at once, Lieutenant Colonel."

"Leave, sir?"

"For now. A personal matter of the utmost importunatcy. My family. Wife and children. I only now am in receipt of word from home. The plague."

"I see. Yes, sir. Of course."

"While I am away, for however long I am away, you, as ranking regular officer here, shall assume command of this place and of its garrison."

"Yes, sir. Of course. As you think wise."

"I do think wise, Lieutenant Colonel, and before I depart I intend to impress upon the men just *how* wise. I am heartily sorry to toss you into the breach this way, son, but have every confidence that you will acquit yourself honorably in the discharge of your duty. By the way, how old *are* you Lieutenant Colonel?"

"Twenty-six, sir. Twenty-seven come summer."

"Ah. Well then, despite my reassurances, I should expect that at some point you are bounden to hear the inevitable grumblings issuing from certain quarters in that respect. My advice? Ignore it as best you can and permit the wisdom of your decisions to speak for itself. By and large these are good, decent, *doughty* men, most of them volunteers here on their own hook who have remained active in our cause despite suffering hardship and deprivation that would have sent lesser men packing long since, indeed did send some 200 packing, fully two-thirds of our complement here, a scant month past. Even so, while some few diehards may be aware of your reputation, they do not know you yet as they know me. All this to say, prepare to be sore-tested."

"Thank you, sir. I pray that I shall meet and master any challenge as it may fall to me after the spirit of your own fine example. So when, sir, should we expect your return?"

"I should think less than a month, Lieutenant Colonel, perhaps a fortnight, no more."

"Very good."

"Until then you shall hold this outpost at all cost. Am I clear?"

"Yes, sir."

"All cost."

"All cost. Yes, sir. Of course. Meaning?"

"I should think Lieutenant Colonel that only time will tell, since time alone determines the measure of all things. Nothing could be clearer than that, if our cause is to crumble, it must only do so upon the barb of time. Borrowed time. Time's speed, son, as you shall come to understand soon enough, is not God's speed. It arrives as it will, passes by swift as horsemen swifter still, and once gone can be redeemed only by the blood of the fighting mad alone."

"Yes, sir. Of course. Time. Blood. Madness. Always of the essence. So hurry back then, sir. *Apresurese atras.* Godspeed on your journey and may you find your family safe, recovered and thriving. Hurry back. At all cost. *Por favor.*"

Bowie

Bowie, which properly is pronounced Boo-ee, not Bo-ee or Bow-ee, greeted me at the ornately-carved double doors of his place in town just off *La Plaza de las Islas* on *Calle Soledad*. This being the former home of his recently deceased father-in-law, Tejas Vice-governor Juan Martín Veramendi.

Ah, Buck, come in, I recall him saying plush-facedly before clutching me by the shoulder by which in turn he tugged me companionably inside. Welcome to *La Casa de Duendes*, Colonel. As they say, *lo que es mío es tuyo*. What is mine is yours. Here. Let's inside, out of the *zaguán*. A shade cool for the garden. We'll pitch camp in the *sala*. I've a fire up and working.

Puffing more maniacally than not on his black cheroot, such dwindling stub as remained, he coughed, then again, something not insignificant catching or obstructing there. And again, yet again. Something stuck, cockleburred in his craw perhaps. Bending over, he grappled with, then gripped his patellas, the tussive coughing, racking him down deep. They sounded hurtful, those coughs, like they must hurt awfully, though they expressed no blood that I noticed, no clots or ropey dislodgements of any sort. Still, he looked....inclement. Hashy.

Uncommonly broad of shoulder, formidable of forehead and cheekbone, near-Romanish of nose and bullish of well-corded neck, his unshaven jaw was a worn-and-torn jut, a *prow* that appeared to have been there and done that, seen it all before and been repeatedly around the roughshod block before coming back for more.

Perdoname, he said, wiping his mouth with the back of a hand while studying at arm's length the indentured cheroot and its ascendant smoke coil.

You should really see to that, I said.

What the *mezcal's* for, he said. Here, and motioned me to sit.

Lowering myself in graduated stages into the intricately embroidered, thick-cushioned chair, I noticed that the carvings of its legs, arms, and back were of a match with those of the massive front doors.

He was clad *en deshabille* in a mustard-colored nightgown and pair of elaborately strappy, hemp-woven *huaraches*. A strong man, I thought to myself, if one no longer so strong as I remembered him from our several encounters back in San Felipe where he had enlisted my offices to see to the thornier details of a number of speculatively problematic, if never less than visionary land grabs. He carried himself now with a *ruined* dignity; nothing could have been clearer than that the glory, if not the fight, had left his once-indomitable body.

The hammered gravel, cobble-floored parlor where we sat—the floor was…crumbly, crusty with sands and granular sediments; you crunched when you walked—was bereft of furniture save our lonely pair of his-and-her chairs, between which stood an oblong end-table atop which squatted his half-filled jar of *mezcal* and the customary *jicara*, the calabash half-gourd from which the liquor ritually is drunk. A tall—six, six-and-a-half, seven-foot—*lophocereus schottii* cactus, dead or momentarily to be, drooped at a severely saddened angle against a wall in a far corner.

He had a mesquite-fed fire roaring in the mantel-less fireplace directly across from us, above which hung an uncommonly large, elaborately framed oil portrait of a decidedly gaunt, but as the expression goes, "beautiful, dark-haired, dark-eyed Spanish maiden," wearing a black dress surmounted by a delicately crocheted, white lace gorget and a winsomely sad, Mona Lisa smile; comely yet melancholic. Squinting with a closed left eye, I measured its breadth and height with a furtive thumb.

A beagle-colored, flop-eared, noticeably flea-bitten *perro* sprawled warming before the fire upon its elongated back, softly snoring. Basset, I believe the breed is called. When Bowie noticed me noticing it, he remarked, "Lucy. Old gal now. Part blind. Deaf as a post. Ursula's from a pup. All I have left. All I have left of her."

I smelled the liquor on his breath, though he did not yet reek of being soaked in it as he so often did; it was no secret that he and Houston often got drunk together. Before becoming too ill to do so, Bowie drank regularly, too regularly. Not that he did not have cause. He had lost more than just his wife and her family when the cholera had taken them. He had lost what he called his "will to love."

I had heard that the place had gone largely to seed since the death of the Veramendis some 30 months earlier. Certainly it no longer was the showplace it once reputedly had been. There were, I noticed, enough cobwebs in evidence to weave a quilt, though as far as I could tell, it was not infested with tarantulas, scorpions, snakes, bats or other, less recognizable vermin. Hives and hibernacles of shadow nested in the corners.

"This house is haunted you know," he said of a sudden. "My wife and in-laws still inhabit the place. I hear them knocking about at night. I don't mind. Find it comforting."

What is haunted, I thought to myself, is Jim Bowie. The attic and cellar of his soul.

Gazing into the flames, their light-throw flickering the features of his face, a face as morose as any I ever had seen, he leaned sharply forward, rocked some in his chair, shook his head. "Goddamn fucking plague! My own Ursula…." He faltered.

"I know," I said. "I *am* sorry."

"Takes it out of you," he said. "Devil's work. Pound of flesh. Takes the best of you with it. Will to love. Kills that off too."

"Pardon?"

"Will to love, Buck, will to love." Glanced then at the portrait, glister-eyed. "All worthwhile there for awhile, while she still…We believe she was with child, you know."

"No," I said. "I did not know."

"Hell of it is, could be I didn't love her when I married her. Not enough. Intended to, wanted to, but it was the opportunity, a proposition, a transaction. I was marrying into her family, you see. But then, well, it became something else. For the both of us. Became…more. And it still was, becoming, more. More of whatever it still was going to become. We'd got past the beginnings and were getting started, re-started, when…"

A silence, one just long enough to be awkward. Apparently he was leaving it to me. "*El cuchillo*," I finally said, unable to cobble together anything more inspired or less insipid, referencing his Florida-sized hand-to-hand combat and/or entrenching tool-*cum*-phallic totem, that legendary, gleaming, 14-inch-long *membrum virile giganticus*.

"Yes?"

"Notice you're not wearing it. Don't think I've ever seen you so naked. So to say."

"No. Never do around the place. Ursula wouldn't have it. Or her folks. Considered it uncivilized. House rules. Got into the habit of going around without. Second nature now. Damn thing's a fucking mortification to lug around all day anyway. First thing I do when I walk through that door"—he nodded in the direction—"unbuckle and unbelt. Feels like getting out of jail. Ever since the Sandbar Scrape. Ever tell you about the Sandbar Scrape, Buck? One helluva to-do, that."

He *had* told me about the Sandbar Scrape. More than once, actually. Countless times, actually. He told anyone who would listen and not a few who wouldn't. And why not? Prior to that "chance medley" duel—more accurately, free-for-all brawl—on that spit of land in the Mississippi up above Natchez almost a decade earlier, he had been little but West Louisiana's shiftiest fortune-hunting slave-trafficker. Subsequent to it, once that four-against-one affray was written up in newspapers from New Orleans to New York City, his reputation as the proverbial man not to be trifled with spread throughout the Southwest. Not that he didn't suffer for his having been twice lungshot, bad skull-fractured, and sword-stabbed seven times, wounds that in a lesser man would have proved mortal upon the spot. Took him a year and a half to recover, and, it was only too apparent, he never had done so fully. Not near.

I sensed that the 40-year-old, reef-wrecked, sodden brig of a man sitting in the chair beside me was disintegrating spanker by spar before my eyes.

"One and only time I ever had need of its use as a fighting weapon," he said. "That farcical one-off dust-up."

"Still," I said, "impressive piece of hardware."

"Oh sure, sure," he said. "Sharp enough for a razor, hard enough for a hatchet, broad enough for a paddle, long enough for a sword. I like to say I keep its blade edge so keen, it cuts through water without getting wet. I had a lady friend once, back in New Orleans, who commented that just to look at it gave her a throbbing case of the sops."

I laughed. "Yes, well, one can only imagine."

"Besides," he said. "Truth? My nerves are about all shot to hell, Buck. Not my nerve, mind. Nerve I've got aplenty, too much maybe. But a man forgets, loses focus, gets distracted, stops paying attention. All it takes is a single slip of the wrist and—slanch!—self-inflicted, you're bleeding out. Lookee here." Lifting his right arm, he held it outstretched before him. Stiff as lumber. Save for the hand. The massive, massively scarred hand which trembled as if palsy-struck. "Is that not," he said, "one helluva fine howdy-do?"

At a loss, I chose to change course. "So, Colonel Bowie, what are we going to do then?"

"Do?" he said, quieting the right hand in his lap, massaging it with his left. "About what, Buck?" Pouring himself some of the *mezcal* and offering me the same, which I waved casually off, he raised the *jicara* in a toast to the portraitured image—*arriba, abajo, al centro, adentro*; up, down, center, within—and tossed it back. Then in swift succession another. And another. "Ah," he said, "there's the steady."

I believed he knew perfectly well about what. "About *la escritura en la pared*, Jim," I said. "About the writing on the wall."

He hesitated a moment, appeared to mull some. "You know why I drink, Buck? I drink for the same reason most people drink—to forget, drown the pain, the hurt, the memories. But you know what? Know what I've learned?"

"What's that?"

"Pain swims."

"Ah," I said, not knowing what else to say until after what I considered an acceptable pause I tried again. "Two matters are most pressing, Jim—command and defense. As you are aware, more than half the men here are volunteers. That's a full four companies over which I have no authority whatever. They are free to stay or go as the spirit may move them, and a good half of them, as you know, have expressed their intention to do the latter momentarily. Nor, with Neill gone, can I say I blame them. They do not know me, and what they may think they know does not cut to my benefit. At best, our situation here is unenviable. At worst, untenable. Were such a depletion to occur now, it would constitute an unmitigated disaster. We are a paltry few as it is. We can ill afford the loss of a single man."

"Agreed," he said, appearing to muse a moment. "There *is* a way around that, you know. To ensure they stick."

"Yes?"

"Election."

"Pardon?"

"Show of hands, Buck. Let them vote in their own head man. Give them a reason to stay. A say. Invest them personally in remaining an active part of our effort here."

"Split command?"

"Share it. Partnership. Co-equal partnership. Two heads better than one."

"They'll vote you."

"Goes without saying." He paused. "Anything to keep those men on board."

His arm was outstretched across the table, hand out. Helluva hand. Callused, nicked, cratered. Gouged. Hideously gouged. Scars layered atop scars. I gripped it in my own.

He said nothing. I said the same. And then I said, not knowing I was about to say it, "WHY? Why didn't you just blow the damn place to Hades, Jim? That fucking Alamo out there, the way Houston wanted, the way he told you? I have no use for that man personally, you know that, but about that papist cesspit, he is correct. It is of no military value whatever. Too far west, too isolated, too exposed. How did he put it to me? 'It is beyond our sphere of influence and safety. If need be, fall back to a more *eligible* position. Blow it to hell, or let the Mex have it.' I know he advised you likewise."

Bowie did not respond save to mutter, "That was a suggestion not an order. That was left to my discretion. Sam Houston is a good man, but Sam Houston is not here. I'm here."

"Fair enough," I said. "But unless we are massively reinforced, *Bejar* is positively indefensible and that Alamo out there is a perfect deathtrap. Twenty-one cannon mounted, each requiring a six-man crew to operate at anything approaching maximum proficiency? We are going to need three, four times the number of fighting men we have at present. Six-hundred minimum, 800 to be comfortable."

Sighing, Bowie leaned back in his chair using its arms to hoist himself more upright, wincing for the effort. "Those cannon," he said, "represent the largest collection of artillery amassed in one spot east of the Mississippi. We hadn't, as we still haven't, the means to remove and salvage them, and I'll be damned if I am going to abandon a bounty like that to Santa Anna or anyone else. That's one. Two, is that contrary to Sam's opinion that the place is of no importance, *Bejar* represents the far-forward frontier piquet guard protecting the route into our interior settlements, and in my considered opinion, holding it represents *la salvación de Tejas*. Which is why, Buck, when I wrote Sam that we would rather die in these ditches than give the place up to the enemy, I was as I am still in dead earnest. To be a Texian is *to wager one's life on staking one's claim*. Simple as that. And three, three Buck"—both hands were clenched tight, balled to fists—"*this…is…my…home!* I live here. I <u>choose</u> to live here and nowhere else."

"Indeed," I said, "as do I. Still, as much as I despise Santa Anna, as much as I detest his government, as much as I have suffered personally at its hands, as much as I love Tejas, Tejas at day's end is theirs. By law."

"Maybe. Technically. For now."

"And that doesn't give you pause? Doesn't, pardon the lawyer talk, mitigate to a degree what we are about here?"

"No, it doesn't."

"No qualms?"

"Why? In what sense? Moral? That's hairsplitting, Buck. No. No qualms. Not one."

"Look, Jim, you know my feelings, but it serves no purpose to pretend that what we are about here is other than strictly illegal. If we succeed, if we pull this thing off, it will be nothing less than the biggest land grab in American history."

"Yes," he said, "it will, and deservedly so. Mexico doesn't deserve to keep Tejas, Buck. She's forfeited all right to her, moral right above all. I've bunked or bivouacked hereabouts for most of a decade, and I can tell you for a damn fact it's always treated her, this territory, like a curb-kicked forgotten cur. Mexico City has no more idea of how to govern Tejas, Buck, than I know how to knit mittens or play the harp."

I smiled. "You sound like Austin," I said. "Often heard him remark, sooner give a loaded pistol to a two-year-old, than endow a Mexican politician with authority. He understands nothing save despotism on the one hand, or anarchy on the other, and given the day of the week or hour of the day, there is no saying which path he may choose to follow. One moment he is for republicanism, the next for fanatical heptarchy, the next for military dictatorship, the next for some jumbled mixture of the most retrograde elements of each."

Bowie smiled back. "Before we moved in, Buck—and let

me be clear, we did not intervene or invade, we didn't show up where we weren't wanted or had no business being, we were encouraged, *invited*, **enticed** in at 12 ½ cents per tax-free acre."

"The fox welcomed into the henhouse, that it?"

"You could say that. Or serpent into the garden, the same garden that same serpent worked tirelessly to make flower, bloom, bear fruit. Before we moved in, Buck, it was nothing. Tejas was nothing. *Una frontera.* The perfect No man's Land. *Un despoblado perfecto.* An enormous ghost town, save that no one ever had bothered to build the town. They wanted us, pleaded with us to reclaim it from *los indios barbaros y tribus salvajes.* 50,000 of them in those days. Comanch, mainly. Fucking centaurs! Killed more Americans per their own number than any tribe on the continent! You aware of that Buck?"

I shook my head.

"And now, after cleaning them out, civilizing things for them, building things up, venturing some capital, applying some elbow grease, risking life, limb and damnation, now after 15 long, hard, damn dangerous years of investing our blood, sweat and tears, the while being obliged to bend over and spread 'em every time Mexico City sprouts a hard-on, now because Santa Anna has his knickers in a knot over how we choose to manage our affairs, he wants not only to kick us out on account, but kill us off?" He shook his head. "No. I don't think so. Not without a fight."

He was wheezing. His lungs sounded graveled, grit scrape on a washboard. I hesitated to say what was on my mind until I found myself saying it. "Afraid?" I said.

"Of what, Buck?" He wiped his lips with the back of his hand.

"I dunno, Jim. Death, I imagine. Dying."

"That?" He almost chuckled. "Nah. No. Not to mention. Too late, Buck, too late for that. After Ursula, I just gave up on it. Not all at once, a little here, a little there, until after awhile….Besides, there's enough to be scared of without being scared of that."

"Tejas," I said.

"What's that?"

"Tejas. Live in her long enough, there's so much of it everywhere around, so much death, a man gets so used to it, scarcely notices anymore. Gets used to it, or gets the hell out. What's it the Mex say? '*La vida nos ha curado de miedo.*' Life has cured us of fear."

Bowie cocked his head and smiled. "Spoken like a true Texian, Buck. So you with me, Colonel? Up for the fight of your life? Prepared to fuck ol' Santa Anna in the ass and leave your big swingin' dick behind as a token of your appreciation?"

I looked hard at Jim Bowie then, looked hard and right on through him. Not that he blinked. He wasn't the blinking sort.

"Fighters," I said evenly, suppressing the impulse to sigh while feeling myself figuratively sighing. "If we are going to do this, Jim, if we are going to have a prayer of doing this, we are going to need to round up every available, able-bodied fighting man in the territory. Is that possible? Can we manage such a thing?"

"I have no idea, Buck." He shrugged. "Does it matter?"

"It might, if the object is to walk away to fight another day."

"And is it, Colonel? In your considered judgment, is that the object here?"

"According to my orders, the object is to hold this position at all cost."

"And so we shall, Buck, so we shall. Hold it. You and I. Together. At *all* cost."

Travis Diary, Feb. 6, 1836:

Useful parley with Bowie. But I worry. Nothing could be more apparent than that his health, already eroded to an alarming extent, may break at any moment. That the man cannot be dissuaded from consuming deplorable amounts of hard liquor is only pitiful—a more ardent sot it would be difficult to imagine—though admittedly there is little I or anyone else can profitably do in that respect. I must only trust that he will remain sober & steady on his feet long enough to effectively meet the challenges he is certain to face in consequence of our new arrangement in joint command. Should he fall too ill to do so, such a blow could well prove mortal. I need him. I need Jim Bowie, have need of his constancy, to be as much of himself entire at all times as he can muster the wherewithal to be. As for our gentleman's agreement, henceforth he shall take tactical charge of our Volunteers while I continue in command of the Regulars, but any strategic decision affecting the garrison as a whole shall be arrived at jointly, by mutual consent and accord. Notwithstanding the man's more glaring deficiencies of character, I pray that we shall find it to the benefit of what we are trying to accomplish here to work together in good faith towards the realization of that object which we both of us hold so dearly deep in common. I cannot help but respect Jim Bowie more than I admire him, but that he is a fighter for *mi Tejas*, for **nuestro Tejas**, of that there can be no question.

Figure & Ground: Cul de sac

The Alamo, at least as it was configured at the time, amounted to little but a walled-in compound enclosing some three acres more or less oblong in shape. It might better be described as a rectilinear polygon, an asymmetrically enclosed, polygonal open space of trampled-flat, relatively level ground after the manner of a sprawling courtyard or plaza, one boxed in on four sides by walls of varying lengths, heights (eight to 20 feet), thicknesses (three to four feet), and angularities.

Composed of locally-quarried limestone augmented with adobe, the shortest of these walls, the ones to the North and South, were 200 to 250 feet long. The longer ones, to the East and West, roughly twice that. All told, some 2,100 rectilinear feet, each one of which required armed defense.

Along the inner side of the walls were located certain contiguous and/or adjacent structures that included perhaps a dozen thatch-roofed *jacale* mud huts—the largest of these, lying midpoint along the West Wall, known locally as the Treviño House, served as my quarters—a series of elongated flat-roofed single-story barracks rooms, a single two-story flat-roofed building called the *Convento* that housed our infirmary, and tucked into the far southeast corner, the ruins of a 30-foot high, cruciform-configured, roofless church (subdivided into chancel, transepts, nave, sacristy, baptistery, confessional, lavatorio and monk's burial chamber) known simply as the Chapel.

This compound perched fully exposed, nakedly isolated upon an elevated river plain or benchland roughly 500 yards east-northeast of the outer edge of the town of *Bejar*, the town center of which, *La Plaza de las Islas*, was designated by the 65-foot-high, octagonal-walled, domed bell tower of the San Fernando Church, reposing some 1,100 yards distant.

Interposed between the compound and the town, intermittently oxbowing and hairpinning at virtual right angles, meandered the *Rio San Antonio*: width, 30 to 100 feet; average depth, four to five feet; temperature, between 68 and 76 degrees Fahrenheit.

This, then, was the approximate morphological and topological lay-out that Santa Anna called "an irregular fortification hardly worthy of the name, a mere corral and nothing more," that our own engineer, Green Jameson, claimed was "never built to be a military fortress," and that I had come to conceive of as *THE BURROW*.

With respect to its function as a fort, the glaring weak point of the place, its breach point, penetration point, the obvious point of attack—I knew it, the Mex knew it, everyone knew it, only a dolt or blind man could have missed it—the one clearly inviting the greatest lethal throw-weight, was *El Pared Norte*. The North Wall.

There, despite Jameson's best berming, bratticing and barbicaning, best barricading, bulkheading and breastworking, there despite his counterscarping denticulated trenching efforts, it remained a degraded shambles. Constructed of local limestone, it was 240 feet long, all of 80 yards, and stood twelve feet high. So, at any rate, reported Jameson, who was hard at work bulwarking it with what he called a "revetted," full-height, two-foot thick, outer facing or facade of excavated earth banked up and braced with tied-and-laddered cross-timbers buttressed with vertical pales.

In effect, it was little more than a reinforced, packed dirt retaining wall, one along the interior midpoint of which he had had his carpenters assemble a hewn-wood platform, a 54-foot-long parapet or rampart which I soon found myself referring to as the "loft-up," it reminding me of the deck of an airborne raft or elevated flatboat.

In fact, it was simply a bed of mesquite wood adzed-and-mattocked sufficiently flat and level enough to effectively mount and emplace cannon. Accessed by a 51-foot-long plankwood ramp raised, according to Jameson, in accordance with the engineering rule-of-thumb of six feet of ramp to every one foot of platform height—the deck, which Jameson called a battery *en barbe*, stood eight-feet-seven-and-a-half-inches in the air and 24 feet front to back. All told, 1,300 square feet. Roomy, if not capacious.

Having knocked out a trio of embrasures in the stone wall for cannon to fire through, Jameson was of the opinion that the wall remained vulnerable even so. I knew it remained vulnerable. Only a dolt or blind man would not have realized that it remained vulnerable. When Jameson told me that wall was in want of further shoring, more elaborate shoring, I could only respond, "Go ahead then, Green. Shore away. What do you need?"

He had his dunnage list ready. Handing it to me, I read: joists, struts and stanchions, girders, I-beams, rebars, sandbags, Kapok bales, riprap, gabions and fascines, cribbing, cinder block, ferro concrete slab. Backfill of any sort: ballast, bags of talus, groynes, ossified sod and ore slag. Asbestos lagging, creped cellulose wadding, molded pulp, corrugated cardboard, white cork. Insulation. Revetment material: window dummies, hollow-core doors, wrought-iron banisters, red catalfalques, styrofoam peanuts, bubblewrap, air pillows, papar, vulcanized bowling balls and Indians pins. HESCO bastion baskets!

I am not, I told him, a specialist in Futurist Procurement. Try to do the best you can with what you have and can manage to scavenge. At which moment, I felt the very soul of stupidity. Vapidity. But then, that is what we rapidly were being reduced to by our reduced circumstances: that which was indisputably necessary, was likewise that which was arrantly preposterous.

The truth was, even at its best, and that best seldom was more than stercoraceous, the place remained redolent of some misbegotten necropolis. A Malebolge, an Evil Ditch, one roosting for the easy pickin's upon a remote, half-savage, aridly sterile outback that collapsed all horizons to the point of implosion.

At last, this fucking, beknighted Alamo was nothing but three acres of compression and claustrophobia, a site of great hate and little room, room within which one sensed oneself sealed up and shut in, in danger at any moment of being deglutitioned—or buried alive. Encrypted-in-vivo.

And should the enemy appear, and there was every reason to believe that, so long as we continued to make noises about defiantly holding onto the place, the enemy eventually must appear, we clearly were going to find ourselves cooped up, boxed in and pinned down inside the very ass-end of the misbegotten, prolapsed world.

Travis Diary, Feb. 8, 1836:

David Crockett is here. The celebrated, the inimitable Davy. Bowie fetched him in late last night from the *Campo Santo*, the papist cemetery west of town where he and his party consisting of four others had gotten hopelessly lost and were waiting abashedly in the rain. We, Bowie and myself, immediately invited him to join in command of this place to which offer he replied, declining, that he is here only to "assist" and wishes to be considered no more than a "High Private." Not that it matters in light of the uneasy particulars of our immediate situation—any pig in a poke, after all, and the men, at least for the moment, do seem rather buoyed by his presence (or its persona)—but, god forgive me my skepticism, I know better than to believe that this self-inebriated if seldom-less-than-shrewd Davy-come-lately is here merely to lend a hand on our behalf. He is here because having latterly been famously defeated in his bid to be re-elected to a fourth term as a U. S. Congressman from Tennessee, he recognizes the opportunity Tejas affords him to re-habilitate both his public reputation and financial and political fortunes. David Crockett. The celebrated Davy. The inimitable Davy. And a party of four. *Four!* Damn! I cannot even count that low.

Fandango

I was out on the dancefloor *zapateado*-ing with the comeliest señorita in all of *Bejar*, comely in that peculiarly sub-tropical, humidly Latin or Castilian way, when I heard Bowie—his rafter-resonant, ophicleide-loud voice was unmistakable—roaring my name.

I was not in the mood for Bowie. Not tonight. And it was one helluva night, a regular making-merry rowdydow. Eating too much, drinking too much, singing and dancing and jawing and chawing and laughing far too much. Breasts grabbed, asses pinched, thighs furtively stroked.

Over there, a convivial bout or two of good-natured arm-wrestling at a carved-up corner table. Over there, a tobaccy spitting contest for both accuracy and distance. Back over there, companionable cockfights to the death. And right here, leashed scorpion races.

Also to be noted were:

colored lantern lights strung as if by clothesline low overhead; they sagged and swagged

aromas of corn foods cooking over mesquite fires; they wended and wafted, emanating

the occasional distant firework; they arc'd and evanesced

the more occasional blackpowder burst of gunfire; they signified war and revelry alike

the incessant barkings and beaglings of pariah packdogs and intermittent yip-yipping of rogue coyote; they resounded, echoing wild and resonantly against the shatterproof night

the thk-thking of maracas, clikket-snicking of *castañetas*, scritching-and-brazzing of *guiros*; they were percussively, if no less infernally insistent

I liked dancing. I not only was good at it, I knew I was good at it. But I did not like parties. I loathed parties. I found parties enervating. I was at this one only because Bowie had talked me into going, persuaded me that my absence would be conspicuous and misconstrued, that the men would interpret it as my thinking myself, "too high and mighty to rub shoulders," as he put it, "with the hoi polloi."

The truth was, I had damn little use for the hoi polloi, but I went anyway, put in an appearance, made the out-of-character gesture. So here I was where I wished I wasn't, dancing up a contrary storm in celebration of the sudden, entirely suspicious arrival of America's foremost folk hero-of-the-moment, who *at* the moment was over there in the corner with the rest of the music-makers, fiddle to chin trying to keep up with their shifting duple and triple metric rhythms, wide grinning the while. The man always was grinning. Irritated the hell out of me.

"You need to hear this, Colonel," said Bowie, tugging me from the dancefloor while flicking the scrap of paper held in his hand with the cracked, noticeably jagged nail of his index finger. "Just in from one of Seguin's boys. Blas Herrara."

Taking it from him, I read. Tried to. Hard squint. A larger load on than I realized. Damn words refused to stay put on the damn paper. Swam like runny yolks on a plate awriggle with worms. I was having real trouble trying to make *cara o cruz*, of what was scrawled there.

"By the way," added Bowie, "Herrara was all beside himself. Seemed spooked."

"You know this Blas?" I asked, aware that I was slightly slurring.

"Herrara? I do," said Bowie. "Seguin's cousin."

"Reliable?"

"As rain. I'll vouch. If he's spooked, likely a good reason."

"So"—this was fucking hopeless; I was at a loss, lost to the lubricant; I handed the paper back to him—"what does it say?"

"Says," he said, not missing a syncopated beat, "that Santana's four days march out of *Presidio de Rio Grande* with 13,000 men. 10,000 foot infantry, 3,000 horse cavalry. Says he's designs on taking *Bejar*. Says," now he was quoting, "he'll be neither delayed nor swayed in single-minded pursuit of his object."

I knew the *Presidio de Rio Grande*. Some called it *Villa de Guerrero*. 150 miles southwest. Which meant—I was calculating it, ciphering, trying to, let's see, a single man on a single horse could, going at a half decent clip, comfortably cover that kind of ground in four days?—with that many men, God knows how many siege cannon, it should take him—what?—at least a fortnight or two to reach us?

"So?" Bowie remarked. Always hyperventilating, Bowie. Always impetuously up and fight-ready aching for *action*. "What plans then? We should council, Buck, pow-wow, make preparations. Not a moment to waste. We should…."

"*Mañana*, Jim," I heard myself saying. "We can do nothing tonight, nothing worth doing, nothing but a lot of headless-chickening around in the damn dark. Tomorrow's another day. Soon enough. We'll put our *cabezas* together, call a council of the officers, *mañana*. Time enough to do what needs doing when we get around to it."

Rolling his cheroot east to west, west to east between his lips before bringing it to a halt with a sudden tooth-clench mid-mouth, Bowie replied, "*Piquet* guards, Buck. We should at least deploy *piquet* guards. Out of town. Roads in. I'll sleep a helluva lot better tonight if we…."

"Fine," I said. "Good. Brilliant. See to it. But right now? Right now I'm dancing with Peach Melba over there and…"

"It always is wisdom, Buck," he said, not yet livid, if half-fuming, "to do that which is necessary before it becomes necessary to do it. Cunctation, Colonel"—he pronounced it kunk-shin—"ever hear of it?"

"Relax, Colonel. Hold your water. You fret too much, don't mind me saying. I'm all for prudence and precaution, but Jesus

Christ on his rosy red cross, what conceivable difference can a few hours make? You know"—I knew I shouldn't say what I knew I was about to say, but the tequila had me saying it anyway—"there are times when you...."

"What?" he interrupted, his glower on. "When what? When I what, Colonel?"

"When you are just so damn....*formulaic.*"

Bowie growled something I failed to catch, coughed blood into his kerchief, snarled and stomped off. I was not surprised. Lately, the man had convinced himself that he was the fucking King of Improvisation, the Prince Elect of Impromptu, *Señor Guerrillero Ultimo,* when in fact he was nothing if not predictably predictable. Predictably the Bayou Boy. Predictably Jimbo. Predictably Bowie.

So tiresome. So tedious. So...all of himself, every active inch.

Besides, I did not believe it. This so-called intelligence, this scuttlebutt, Herrara's report. Not all of it anyway. I had little doubt that Santa Anna might be on the move, but that he was already at *Guerrero* with 13,000 and heavy cannon in the dead of winter? No, that I could not credit.

Now, I knew that Herrara was Seguin's man, and I knew that Seguin could be trusted. Johnny Seguin was one mighty fine *hombre.* Stand-up as they come. Loyal to a fault and an exemplar of his kind, one whose hatred of Santa Anna, although of a different quality, I knew exceeded even my own. But we had had our false alarms before, oodles of them. Before the night was out, it would not have surprised me had there been reports that S.A. himself had slipped in and out of the damn shindig disguised as a damn priest. Lately, the paranoia in *Bejar* was rampant. Everyone was seeing ghosts, *fantasmas,* monsters under every *cama.*

In any event, even should the information, unlikely as it was—for the weather had turned, the distance was far, the topography both unfriendly (being bereft of forage, virtually so of water, all but impassable with rutty bad roads) and Comanch-ridden—even should the report prove accurate, I estimated that we had, realistically, at least another three to four weeks, likely many more, before we needed to be overly concerned.

I headed back out onto the dancefloor thinking, *mañana. Mañana's* soon enough. For the moment all I wanted, all I wished, all I intended, was to disappear inside the rhythms of the *huapango*. Fandango the *noche* away, lost, oblivious, until the very risen sun.

Travis Diary, Feb. 11, 1836, 4 a.m.:

Stupid party! Frivolous I can be, am capable of being, when frivolity is called for, when it is fitting, but frivolous I decidedly choose not to be when cultivating the distance required to wait for dreams that seldom come true not to come true, reckoning, widdershins, whether dreams are for a reason and why it is that the dreamer cannot wash this night from his eyes weep wonderstruck as I may. *Borracho. Muy borracho.* I'll pay this day. There are moments, latterly more moments, when I feel like Job himself. As if my soul is weary of my life, the weariness of having lived it. Sampling it as I sleepwalk, before spitting it out in disgust. These moments when my life feels like nothing so much as preparation for its imminent end. Twenty-six years old and <u>superfluous</u>! As superfluous to myself as I suspect I always have been to others. *Better go slaughter one's own kind in the name of peace....there's small dancing left for us any way you look at it.* Ach! Drunken thoughts. Enough. To bed.

Travis Diary, Feb. 16, 1836:

55 degrees. As a result of the meeting of our officer corps here, I have dispatched Lieutenant Bonham with appeals to all quarters. Much hinges on his success in rousing the settlements to send on to us men and arms in the most timely fashion possible. All pray that he may meet with a serious, immediate, active, and, most importantly, massive response. Bonham is a favorite here. I much favor him myself. 6'2", 29 years old, ox-strong and handsome as Apollo, a fellow South Carolinian and silver-tongued lawyer of the highest character. Bowie and I agree that he is the one man head-and-shoulders best suited to succeed in carrying out this most sacred mission. If the dauntless James Butler Bonham, whose steadiness of nerve is exceeded only by his staunchness of spirit, cannot persuade our brethren to march at once to our succor, no man can.

May God goddamn anyone who ever prayed for peace,
or preached a word of compassion!

(William B. Travis, from the Alamo,
to Stephen F. Austin, in Nashville, 2/20/36)*

*(As "Texas Commissioner to the United States," Austin
had left for Washington D.C. before the end of the year
charged with negotiating a $1 million federal loan, soliciting
contributions from well-heeled private donors, and wooing
public support for the coming war for Texas independence.
Arriving in Nashville the second week in February, he
was in Washington by the last week in March, and, after
stops in Baltimore, Philadelphia and New York City, was
back in Texas on June 27th . Six months later to the day,
having in the meanwhile lost the election to become the
first popularly elected president of the new independent
Republic of Texas to Sam Houston, Stephen Fuller Austin,
age 43, died of pneumonia. Houston lived another 27 years,
leaving at his death an estate worth upwards of $90,000,
including a dozen slaves.)

February 23rd

Notice from afar this call to slaughter...
Harken to the brazen skirls
that rebuke the latecomers
unequipped for battle...

By the time the enemy, or as I then conceived of him, "The Unholy Beast," entered *Bejar* to the church bell chime issuing from the San Fernando Cathedral, most of the town's *Tejano* inhabitants had in advance wisely fled or prudently gone to ground, while we in something resembling organized chaos had withdrawn catch-as-catch-can inside the walls of the Alamo, or as I then conceived of the ruined structure, "The Burrow."

From my vantage post atop the West Wall, I gnawed absently on a *piloncillo oscura*, a conical thimble of hardened brown sugar, while observing through my field glass the commotive, colorfully martial goings-on.

Through my head, thoughts stampeded like herds of headless horses, one of them being, "Well now, appears likely we've overstayed our welcome":

I leap upon the wall trying to grasp all the possible consequences that this turn of events must bring with it. I feel as if we never really organized The Burrow adequately for defense against attack. I had intended to do so, but the danger of an attack, and, consequently, the need to organize the place for defense always seemed so remote. Many things in this direction might have been done, should have been done, but, incomprehensibly, have not been done.

The thing to do now is to go carefully over The Burrow and consider every possible means of defending it. Devise a plan of defense and corresponding plan of construction, then begin the work at once with all the vigor of youth. That is the work that is really needed, the work for which I fear it is now far too late in the day.

I let everything slide. I have been negligent. Derelict in my duty. But no. Stop. That is not helpful. Self-recrimination is not helpful. I need calm the conflict roiling within me. I must not surrender to it, but hurry on. I do not know what I want. Probably simply to put off the hour.

Inconceivable to me is the size and capacity of The Beast, its freshness and vigor, its unceasing single-minded focus on overcoming its object, *us*, which it has the ability to achieve with ease. I could not have foreseen such an opponent. What is happening now is something I should have feared all along, something I should have prepared for, been constantly preparing for, the fact of The Beast's coming. Could I have done something to divert it from its path, forced it to make a wide detour around The Burrow? No. Stop. Too late, too late for that. Why have I been spared so long only to be delivered to such terrors now? Compared to this, what do all the petty dangers I have brooded over in my life amount to?

It is precisely this that I should have foreseen. I should have thought of the defense of The Burrow. Above all, I should have arranged to cut off inner sections of The Burrow, partition them, as many as possible, from the more endangered exposed sections which, when attacked, must inevitably be breached. Not the slightest attempt have I made to carry out such a plan. Nothing at all has been done in that direction. I have not lifted a finger. I have been as thoughtless as a child. I have passed my manhood's years in childish games. I have done nothing but play with the thought of danger. I have shirked my responsibilities, failed to take seriously the real actual danger. It is not as if there has been a lack of warning.

On my side, everything is worse prepared for now than ever. The Burrow stands defenseless, and the powers I still have must only fail me when the decisive hour comes. I cannot endure this place. All my surroundings seem filled with agitation, to be looking at me, through me. The eyes of the walls are angry with accusation and rebuke. They reproach me for a fool. I shake my head. I have not yet found any solution.

I try to unriddle The Beast's plans. Perhaps an understanding with it might be possible, though that cannot, of course, be brought about by negotiation, only by The Beast itself, or some compulsion exercised from my side. In both cases, the decisive factor will be what The Beast knows about me, about us.

Lying in my heap of earth, my Burrow, I can naturally dream all sorts of things, even of an understanding with The Beast, though I know well enough that no such thing can happen, and that at the instant when we see each other—more, at the moment when we sense each other's presence—we shall blindly bare our claws and teeth, neither of us a second before or after the other, both of us raging with a new and different hunger.

Now the noise is growing louder, and this growing-louder is like a seismic coming-nearer. I give the order. The ground judders with thunder; cannon-roar.

Some noise can be seen.

(As a rule, it does little good to run from one's enemy. In my experience, all that one accomplishes in doing so is to fly into the jaws of another. Certainly there are exits. Exits exist. Escape routes. Points of egress. Ways out. Each of which lead to precisely the same place: nowhere. Better to batten down, then. Better, deep, to burrow in. *"Burrow, burrow, burrow! There's a sky that way too if the pit's deep enough so the stars tell us."*)

Travis Diary, evening, Feb. 23, 1836:

52 degrees. Damp. Enemy here in force. His clear design, to take us by surprise, catching us napping while still indolently billeted throughout *Bejar*, was sorely disappointed owing to our *Tejano piquets*, Seguin's boys, who duly alerted us to his presence when still five miles south of town, time enough by several hours to organize and withdraw behind the walls here. I have sent on Mr. Sam Maverick to alert the settlements eastward of our need for immediate reinforcement. At evening's tarnish, the enemy raised his red flag of "no quarter" from the belfry of the San Fernando church in town. I immediately ordered the gesture met with a shot from our 18-pounder mounted at the southwest corner of the compound. Having had time to ruminate and reassess, I now deeply regret having done so. A hasty, impulsive, impetuous and ill-advised, wholly *childish* response not worthy of me or of the men. What could have possessed me? What was I thinking? Am I really possessed of so much hubris? How often we astonish ourselves when put to the test! How often we fail! This gulf between who we are and who we aspire to be. My godforsaken obsession with honor at a time and in a place incompatible with it. Yesterday there was not much wrong. The day before there was not much wrong. Last night there still was not much wrong. Even this morning, not much wrong. But now, now is now, and now everything is wrong, and will remain wrong henceforth. I surmise.

See them? The carvers out there queued up to do their surgery? Carnivores, the lot, wearing their absent scruples like weaponry:

Muskets	(Brown Bess)
Rifles	(Baker)
Carbines	(Paget)
Pistols	(Tower)

Bayonets (17-inch &c), *lanzas* (8-8 ½ foot &c), curved sabers,
    straight swords
Grenades and Congreve Rockets, mortars, howitzers
Canister, shotted grape, solid and shell
Felling axes, crowbars, scaling ladders, rams (&c)
(You must pardon me, please, while I puke.)

I suspect that what awaits us are the shrapnels of hell
But then
Men die miserably everyday for want of a few new words
Anyway.

So remind me. A rising tide lifts what? Again? Exactly?
The moltens that blind the seasickened eye
Churned wall-high
Vaster than the vision of vultures?

So much depends upon
               all that I think
                      being all that I see.

Now it begins: Tick. Tock.

(...history returns, and so can I,
having told myself these things.
And keeping them in readiness to tell again.)

So events, as events will, had taken an irreversible, entirely predictable turn for the, I hesitate to say diabolical, but certainly the gothic. Speaking omnisciently. Out of school. At narrative distance. Possessed of just that brand of faux clarity that too often stems from the illusion that clarity at such moments matters more than does shitting oneself in horripilating fear of catching a bayonet fuck in the neck.

No. The ones too soon to come would, I suspected, be but moments but slantwise glimpsed. *Hoy aqui, mañana se va,* insofar as one might count upon *mañana* arriving at all, the very one that is promised, after all, to none of us. This geometry of fracture. The way any battle shatters proprioception.

Life is grotesque when it is imprisoned inside a story, much less one hijacked by the leitmotivs of history. It is grotesque anyway, any *which* way, but doubly so then, since thought as it relates to memory inevitably is selectively anachronistic. But then memory would be of little use were it factually accurate, since it is in the re-collected inaccuracies—omissions, conflations, compressions, refractions, avulsions, transversions, blurrings and warpings and cantileverings, unwitting elisions and embellishments—and in their re-arranged patchworked permutations and re-sequenced juxtapositions, that our true identity reposes.

It is precisely the forgetting of our history that makes us ourselves. Real selves. Who we really are. Human selves. Fatigued, flawed, forgetful selves. The ones jigsawed of fraught, fallible, fascicled memory. Too fickle, feckless, fa/cet/ed memory.

So much must be forgotten to remember anything at all.

History can only be compromised history. Counterfeit history. Ersatz history. One incomplete version in the moment among other incomplete versions in other moments.

Imposters each, forever revising themselves disfigured by their after-the-fact re-configuration, since memory always arrives in *flashes* coming forward from, not in calibrated *steps* going backward to. Memory emerges, it does not retrieve, much less spit out its facsimilies stamped, dated and framed tidily in that timeless context absent which there can be no real meaning.

Memory is not knowledge, hindsight never 20/20. The mind's eye altering, alters all, to paraphrase Blake, who knew what my mother also knew—that to remember clearly, "use your eyes to *forget*." Because it is only when one comes dumb to the names of what one is looking at, only when the eye is stunned by that which it is looking at, only when the eye "sees strange, unfamiliar, fresh, when it *wonders*, disbelieving," only then "that it sees <u>true</u> what it sees, and not what it thinks it sees," what the mind has accustomed it to seeing.

And even then. Even then to understand that nothing that one sees, *means* what one is seeing. Explains it. Can explain it. Ought be expected to explain it.

Post mortem, ex post facto, the moribund discarded pieces, the bloodless orts of what little is preserved, is preserved as mummy, mock-up, masque, relicts of ambered artifact stuffed and reshaped for display as trophies mounted upon a wall. Chapelyard wall.

We glimpse them there. So much taxidermy.

Compositioning that which is decomposed. Transmuting ash to strokes of ink. Would be alchemy. An aesthetic exercise. The performing of a form. Of darkest magic.

Let us vow an end to *his*-story-telling then. Let us lift from his grave, my grave and yours, the available poetry.

(life is grotesque when we catch
it in *quick* perceptions—
at *full* vent—history
shaping itself)
….in *collage* with time

Travis Diary, Feb. 24, 1836:

53 degrees. Word circulates that today is S.A.'s 42nd birthday; so *feliz cumpleaños, Señor Diablo,* and may it, god willing, prove your last. Word arrives as well that Colonel Bowie is collapsed, that the fever and bloody black flux have left him too weak to rise from bed. I am told that he vomits regularly, vomits green, vomits buckets, is sunk sidewise in delirium. Because our doctor, Pollard, fears contagion, we have arranged to quarantine him in a barrack room along the South Wall east of the Main Gate. There he is nursed with arnica compresses by his sister-in-law, the selfless Mrs. Juana Alsbury. In consequence, our short-lived experiment in shared command is ended. His words to me not some two hours past uttered in a croaking, ecclesiastical whisper were, "It is all on you now Buck. Do not fret. I know these men. They will follow you into hell." My words to him, this festered soul whose lungs I fear now are less filled with the fresh air of liberty than fraught with the cancers of regret, my words to him likewise were, "Let us pray, Jim, that it does not come to that." Nor, frankly, do I believe that it will. We will be succored because we <u>must</u> be succored. If we are not, and soon, Bowie is correct—hell awaits. (I had thought to deposit with him our single Nock Gun, but considered that doing so would only mean squandering it upon a man too weak to wield it, its seven braze-clustered barrels of .52 calibre firepower. Perhaps I shall keep it for myself, this weapon we have taken affectionately to calling, "the Hellblaster." Something whispers to me that I may yet have need of it.) Meanwhile, as we are running perilously low on water, we have taken to rigging up sluiceways and

catchbasins while praying for rain and sending out nightraids to the pond to our west. Whether six at night or three in the morning, the men can see the flicker-glow of my candle through the open window of my billet midpoint along the West Wall, the same window through which they can hear the unceasing scritch of my quill. It is, I suspect, a sound that can only rankle them almost as much as does the enemy's relentless cannonade. I am not so oblivious that I fail to understand that they think me at best an inkhorn, at worst a feckless fop. What kind of man is it, they can only wonder, who seems never to sleep while subsisting on little but pot after pot of black coffee? A man who would place more stock in the written word than he does in their welfare? Who prefers the company of his words, to that of his men, and labors longer over the recursive construction of his sentences, than he does the re-construction of the North Wall? And, in truth, I have squidded the world with enough ink to blue and black the sky twice over. Perhaps, it would not surprise me, they believe that what I have in mind is to language the enemy into abandoning its siege. Narrate it into submission. Poem it to death. Would/ that I/could.

uill in hand, I sat ensconced at my desk in my West Wall quarters composing by wicklight whatever came to me as it came to me to compose it. In fact, it all but composed itself. It, I sensed, was much composing me.

This, what I was about here, was important. More, it was critical. Not to the world, of course, but to us. To those of us, that is, who composed *us*. To we paltry, beleaguered few, nothing could have been more so. Everything—life, death, *love*—hinged upon it.

And so, if I began to think too long or too deeply about what I was writing—more to the point, what was writing itself—if I permitted my brain to intervene, to *meddle*, I knew that I was going to lose control of it, the flow of it, by endeavoring to control my lack of control of it.

A great discipline, you see, self-discipline, the discipline to step aside, to *let go*, was involved in this sort of composing, in its shaping the shape it insisted upon shaping upon the page. The way it unfolded there, unfurled itself to its fullest, most fully manifested unfurling, as if my quill was a chisel and the composition a sculpture developed angle by line from some block of virgin granite. The shapes—remarkable!—floated up, lifted, drifted to the surface emerging gouge by gouge, chip by chip, flake by quillstroked flake.

And I knew, I did not know just how I knew, but I knew, had never been so certain of anything in my life, I knew that if I stopped now, if the writing stopped, I would become a lie. My entire life, a fiction.

Commandancy of the Alamo
Bejar
Feby. 24th, 1836

To the People of Texas & All Americans in the World—
Fellow Citizens & Compatriots—

I am besieged by a thousand or more of the Mexicans under Santa Anna—I have sustained a continual bombardment & cannonade for 24 hours & have not lost a man—The enemy has demanded a surrender at discretion otherwise the garrison is to be put to the sword if the fort is taken—I have answered the demand with a cannon shot & our flag still waves proudly from the walls—*I shall never surrender or retreat.* Then I call upon you in the name of liberty, of patriotism, of everything dear to the American character to come to our aid with all dispatch—The enemy is receiving reinforcements daily & will no doubt increase to three or four thousand in four or five days. If this call is neglected I am determined to sustain myself as long as possible & die like a soldier who never forgets what is due to his own honor & that of his country.

VICTORY or DEATH

William Barret Travis
Lt. Col. Comdt.

Slotting the quill in its inkwell, I went back, read over what I had written, re-read it, word by word, read it again, then aloud, then to myself, a third time, a fourth.

No. Decidedly not. Something was wrong. Off. Something was missing.

If the words were far from the worst I ever had committed to paper, still, they would not do. They fell flat, far short of where they needed to fall. Inadequate, insufficient, infested with pleonasms, superfluities, with the bacilli and spirochetes of incursive foreign bodies. I could not put my finger on them, could not pinpoint, but no, they would not do, not at all. They did not work the way I needed them to work, the way they had to work, if they were to work.

I decided to underscore VICTORY or DEATH twice more, to furnish the phrase—fine phrase if a tad overdramatic (though if ever there were an occasion when a little melodrama was called for, surely, I thought to myself, this could only be it)—with more *kick*, some additional oomph, in triplicate.

Better, yes. But still, no.

Fisting the paper to a ball, I dropped it dismissively—no, disdainfully, no, contemptuously—to the floor. Then, at no little length, after an elongated moment, several seconds of second thought, I reached down, retrieved it, uncrushed it, smoothed it face up across the desktop ironing out its creases.

Holding one corner, top left, over the tallow flame, I studied it as it singed some, caught, curled, crimped, was consumed with flame, the fire spreading in a scorch that blackened the flattened paper even as it crumpled to an ash-crepe that floated away in flakes falling in featherings to the floor; these wisps of wordless black confetti.

Lost words. Lost words well lost.

Picking up the quill again, I started over, began again. To write. Re-write. To get right what so stubbornly insisted upon being gotten so wrong. To bare, at last, the cat's claw contained occluded in the calamus. To hear aright, for pity's sake, if no other, the proper purring of the page.

Seguin

When I spotted Captain Juan Seguin sprinting past the open door of my West Wall quarters, I welled my quill, sprinkled a dash of silica across the paper upon which I had been writing as if scattering a handful of birdseed, gingerly shook off the excess, carefully slid the sheet from my desktop, rose to my feet and strode beneath the lintel out through the threshold, calling, "Juan! *Capitán* Juan Seguin! *¡Ven acá! Necesito hablar contigo.* I need to speak with you."

"*Sí, mi Coronel. Este canon es…*"

"*Tranquilo, Capitán.* Let them launch their potshots as they will. Haven't singed a hair on a single of our *vasos* yet. *Ni uno.*"

It could only have been *Jueves,* Thursday. Night three of the siege. The enemy's cannonade, as it had been since its arrival, had been an on-again on-again affair, day and night nonstop, siesta time notwithstanding. No surprise, then, that its hammering had begun to grate on more than a few nerves, though the worst any of us had suffered to date was a few cuts and bruises from random flying rockchips.

Now, if *Bejar* could have been said to have a First Family, it was the Seguins. Johnny's grandfather, Santiago, had been one of the town's founding fathers over a century ago. His father, the 53-year-old open border advocate, Don Erasmo, was its first postmaster, quartermaster and mayor, organized its first public school, had been Tejas's sole representative to Mexico's Constitutional Convention some 12 years earlier, and as proprietor of the nearby 31,000-acre *Ranchero de Casa Blanca,* was one of the territory's largest landowners. In the words of Stephen Austin, "Were it not for the good offices of Don Erasmo, our colonies would have died *en útero.*"

"*¿Cómo te va, Juan?*" I asked. "*¿Cómo llevas?* How are you holding up?"

"*Esta bien, mi Coronel. Bellas. Estoy bien.*"

When a shell burst out in the plaza, not far to our left, hailstoning the space with jagged rockshard, I noticed Seguin wince and cross himself.

"*¿Y sus hombres?*" I asked. "*¿Cuántos son en última cuenta ahora?* How many are your men at last count?"

"*Veinticuatro, mi Coronel.* Two dozen. *Están bien así.*"

"Glad to hear it *Capitán, porque* as I believe I have made clear, I do not like this *elecciones* business, your having been voted by the men to deliver to the world outside our walls news of the inclining hopelessness, *la desesperanza de montaje* of our situation.

"Not that I think you incapable, Juan. To the contrary. *En mi opinion*, no man here is more capable. If anyone has a chance, *una oportunidad* of making it through the enemy's lines unscathed, I have no doubt, none at all, that it is *tu.*

"*Pero*, that is precisely the point. I know *sus hombres* are loyal to you, *leal* unto the very *muerte*, but—*y perdoneme* my bluntness *Capitán, mi franqueza*—once you are gone, need I be concerned that they will they remain loyal to our cause here? My own influence with them, after all, cannot begin to approach your own, and Colonel Bowie's, whose can, is far too ill to exercise it.

"I scarcely am insensitive to the fact that you and your men find yourselves at, shall we say, cross-purposes these days, lodged between the proverbial rock and its hard place, *el diablo y el profundo azul*, damned if you do, damned if you do not."

"*Puedo garantizar nada, mi Coronel*," said Seguin. "I can guarantee nothing. *Pero, debo decir la mitad.* I should say half. *La mitad* will stay and fight."

"*Esta bien*," I said. "Thank you for your candor, *Capitán.* Still, to spare you just now is a great sacrifice. *Un gran sacrificio.* I should want you here close by should the occasion arise that I need to parley with Santa Anna. There is no one I trust more to wring from my words, *mis palabras*, their **full** meaning, *su significado completo*, account for their **every** nuance, *todos los matices*, every intonation and inflection, than yourself."

"*Gracias, mi Coronel, muchas gracias.*"

"Now, Juan, I shall be wanting you to take Bowie's *caballo*. He has no more use for her and she is the best in the fort, so they say. A skewbald named Blaze. And let us pray that she lives up to her *nombre.*"

"*Pero, Coronel,* I have my own. She is not the *más rapido, es verdad, pero…*"

"Blaze, Juan. You will take Blaze. Try Gonzales first. He should be there. If not, they will know where he is. But you must find him, *Capitán.* You must find General Houston. Everything depends upon your doing so, and with all right alacrity, *con todos los celeridad adecuada.*

"I cannot emphasize enough, Juan, *tu es nuestra esperanza última, mejor y único.* You, *tu y tu solo,* are our last, best, our only hope. Each of the couriers I have dispatched over the past fortnight, all the many appeals I have penned, for all it has profited us I might as well have written each one in *agua* upon these *paredes.*"

"*Sí, mi Coronel,*" said Seguin. "Consider it done. *¡Mision complida!*"

"Here then," I said, handing him the dispatch. "Guard this with your life, *con su vida.* Deliver it *sano y salvo,* safe and sound. *Vaya con Dios, Vaquero. Y que los santos a mantenerse a salvo. Dios los bendiga, Juan Seguin.*"

The Plea

To: Major-General Sam Houston,
whereabouts unknown
From: The Commandancy,
H.Q. of the Fort of the Alamo, *Bejar*

Sir,
At present I have 200 men here <u>más</u> <u>o</u> <u>menos</u>. The
enemy has between three & six thousand who presently
encircle us on all sides. It is critical therefore that all aid
be hastened to me with due <u>presteza</u>, **<u>AHORA!</u>** even
as I am determined come what may to hold out to the
last extremity, <u>hasta</u> <u>el ultimo</u> <u>extremo</u>. I have held out,
am holding out still, will, god willing, continue to hold
out so long as there remains a breath in my body, but,
Sir, I cannot hold out much longer.

If I am overpowered, if this place is overrun, those
of us who fall a sacrifice at the shrine of our country,
<u>el santuario</u> <u>de</u> <u>nuestro</u> <u>país</u>, demand—nay, cry out
in reproach from our graves—that our memory be
afforded justice.

I have fortified this place & will continue to fortify it as
I am able to which efforts may rightly be ascribed our
having thus far lost not a single man & this despite by
last count there having fallen inside our works no less
than 217 shells. The enemy's bombardment continues
night & day without let-up or lull.

I wish I could report, Sir, that the spirits of my men
remain doughty & high but despite my most animated
efforts they are in fact plunged in the infernal depths
of such melancholy as I seldom have witnessed. The

mood here surpasses mere gloom. It now is devilish dark & hourly only deepens.

I rely, Sir, upon you alone for aid & unless it arrives soon I shall be left no alternative but to fight the enemy upon his own terms. But while I will not shrink from doing so with the determined valor, dauntless vigor & desperate courage exemplified by our forefathers at Lexington & Concord, at Valley Forge, upon the fields of Chalmette Plantation & while I am confident that my men however dispirited at present will when the moment of the Last Struggle ensues acquit themselves honorably though they be sacrificed upon the vengeful altar of a most **gothic** enemy whose victory I vow to render so dear that much as General Pyrrhus's at Asculum it will augur worse for him than defeat, still it is impossible to overstate the necessity of your flying to our defence **upon the instant.**

Should this be effected with right dispatch this neighborhood may yet be cleansed of an enemy who would sooner murder en masse its inhabitants & render of <u>mi Tejas querido</u>, <u>un desierto residuos perfecto,</u> than cede them their earned & rightful place in this the adopted land of their heartsong's choosing. How much better you must agree to meet the enemy here & now than to suffer later his savaging unto the smoke of the burning dwellings & keening of the famished children of our settlements in the colonies where abideth our most precious mothers, wives, sisters, daughters & innocent babes.

Presently a blood-red banner waves ominously from the church of <u>Bejar</u> betokening the enemy's resolve to put to the sword all "rebels & pirates"—for such is how it pleases him to slander us—should we fail to surrender at discretion. I will not surrender. His threats have no influence on me save to further steel my own resolve to fight with the high-souled courage of the patriot willing to die like a warrior in defense of his own honor & that of his country & if it should fall to my lot to be abandoned here, left a bloody martyr to the indifference of my fellowman, I shall accept it as my fate however unmerited.

For the past 24 hours despite a cramping of my hand so disabling that I am scarce able to grip my quill I have been engaged <u>muy</u> <u>furioso</u> in writing to the people of Gonzales, of San Felipe, of Goliad, of Refugio, of Washington-on-the-Brazos, as well as <u>a</u> <u>la</u> <u>Gente de</u> <u>Tejas</u> <u>y</u> <u>Todos</u> <u>los</u> <u>Americanos</u> <u>en</u> <u>el</u> <u>Mundo</u>. Meanwhile the enemy continues to approximate his works to ours. Each hour he inches closer & I have every reason to apprehend an attack in force at any moment. Therefore, Sir, I implore you by happy home & altar free to heed our plea & hasten on all assistance—as your duty no less than simple humanity demands—in the name of <u>La Sagrada Causa</u> so dear to us all.

Rally to our relief boys! Give me help, O my country! Or let the deaths of those friends & neighbors you deemed fit to forsake in their hour of direst need haunt you for what remains of your <u>días</u> <u>disminuyó</u> even as my words & **the ash of the bones with which they were written** rebuke you & my country for your cruel neglect & the callous **indifference** that murdered us all.

I have instructed the bearer of this appeal should he succeed in escaping through the enemy's lines to provide more detail inclusive of the prostration of Col.

Bowie, latterly my co-commander here.

We remain as one body united a band of brothers, a single crew bound heart & hand to resist until our bodies & properties lie coffered in one common ruin.

Should you fail us, we are lost.

God and Tejas! **<u>Victory or Death!!</u>**

Here the North Wall
and there the Near Wall
and here the South Wall
and there the Far Wall
and here the East Wall
and there the Opposite Wall
and here the West Wall
      reading what is written in tears
      upon each in their turn:

> *No way out, a thousand ways in,*
> *Abandon hope, all ye who enter here*

That which in inclining distress we witnessed day after day in every direction was their incrementally:

Boxing the Compass
Cinching the Circle
Barring the Door

Tuesday, February 23: arrival in *Bejar* of Santa Anna and the Mexican Army; excavation of an artillery battery site west across the river to the rear of the Veramendi *palacio*; cavalry units are deployed to the north and east

Wednesday, February 24: a river battery is established (two 5-inch howitzers, two 8 lb. cannon, one mortar) 300 yards southwest of our West Wall; excavation of a second artillery battery south in *La Villita*, a suburb of *Bejar*

Thursday, February 25: a *La Villita* battery (two cannon) is established 600 yards south of our South Wall; cavalry units are posted along all eastwardroads

Saturday, February 27: the *La Villita* battery is moved up, 300 yards from our South Wall; excavation of a third battery site along the *acequia,* the aqueduct to the northeast

Sunday, February 28: the *acequia* battery is established (two cannon) 500 yards northeast of our North Wall

Monday, February 29: two infantry battalions join with the cavalry sealing off all roads eastward; S.A. declares a three-day armistice during which he offers "life to all defenders who surrender their arms and retire paroled under oath not to take them up again against Mexico."

Tuesday, March 1: trenches are excavated beyond the North
Wall

Wednesday, March 2: our hidden courier route to the east is
discovered and blockaded

Thursday, March 3: the *acequia* battery is moved nearer the
North Wall "within musketshot"; trenches are dug
nearer the North Wall; another 1,000 *soldados* arrive in
Bejar; artillery is consolidated on three sides, north,
south and west

Friday, March 4: the northern artillery batteries, augmented by
two additional howitzers, are moved within 200 yards of
the North Wall; a third cannon is added to the western
battery; (I do **not** draw a line in the sand)

Saturday, March 5: Mexican assault troops deploy to assigned
field positions; the cavalry deploys in force along all
potential escape routes; (I again **decline** to draw a line,
declaring myself opposed in principle to, "publicity
stunts.")

    Earlier that evening, while out strolling amongst the men, I
eavesdropped on an exchange along the walls:
    A: "Do this mean what I think it do?'
    B: "I'm a-feared it do. It means they aim to run weaponized
rings around us, counting on us to be too lame literal-brained to
imagine what's in store."
    A: "That being?"
    B: "That being that time is all on their side. That being that
they'll just keep on a-coming, jockeying closer for position. That
being we're powerless to stop 'em 'til they send in their damn
clowns armed to their damn greasepaint eyes."

B: "I hate clowns. They're not funny, they're creepy. They give me the galloping willies."

A: "Everyone hates clowns."

B: "Still, ain't no laughing matter."

A: "Oh, I dunno. Not at the moment, maybe, but wait awhile. Times to come, there's them in their future like to find it the fucking height of fucking hilarity."

A: "Think?"

B: "I do."

A: "And that should put a smile on my face?"

B: "Nah. It should just keep you from blowing your brains out."

C: "For now."

Travis Diary, Feb. 28, 1836:

40 degrees. Drizzle. Jameson continues his work
upon our defective North Wall, vets it with all care
and consideration, even, dare I say, affection. <u>Exalts</u> in
the baroque improvisations of its restoration. These
superhuman labors to keep even with the damage done,
the collapses and cave-ins effected by the enemy's artillery
which outpaces his efforts at repair. The man and his crew
are indefatigable. On they go by torch and lantern light,
brawn and brain, beavers at their beavering mending what
has been dismantled. Yesterday I spied him upon the wall
scrutinizing the horizon for any sign of intelligent life and,
detecting none, turning back to his men, perhaps spying
less. I find myself now fallen increasingly prey to spending
inordinate blocks of time time-traveling the passageways
of that most savage and inhospitable of all climes—my
own mind. There, at one amidst the cenotes and hypogea,
the constellation of unmapped and unmappable cunicular
corridors, I have discovered that death—young death in my
case, sudden violent death—is lined up eager to pounce;
chupacabra. I recall my mother's words, unintelligible
to me at the time, that life is little but a bust, "a load
of damn rubbish masquerading as a miracle." A man,
I reckon, can turn his back and pretend not to see, but
he does so alone and uncared for through eyes that hurt
more than he can say. Nothing to fear here but nothing,
more nothing, the inclining nothingness. Meanwhile, the
written words of my dispatches are, apparently, considered
by their considerers as little but cornball cheap theatrics,
and my plea for aid and succor dismissed as trafficking in
gross hyperbole and the politics of petty posturing. Damn
Houston! Damn him to perdition!

Fannin

Some 90 miles to our south and east, in the town of Goliad, sat the *Presidio La Bahía*, yet another frontier papist mission-cum-fortress. Its garrison of 300 to 400 "provisionals"—one heard conflicting numbers—chafed, so the rumor, under the high-handed command of one James Walker Fannin, the bastard-born, 32-year-old, slave-trading syndicalist and West Point dropout who fancied himself, as he more than once had boasted in my presence, "the best artillerist in Texas."

Perhaps he was. I honestly could not have said. I knew Fannin some, and knowing what I knew, knew enough to know that not everything he said, particularly about himself, ought be accepted at face value.

What interested me more than Fannin's fondness for brag, however, were his men. We needed them, desperately. *Aqui.* Here. *Ahora.* Now. *Ayer.* Yesterday. I needed Fannin to march his 300 or 350 or 400 men northward, instanter. Not that that number alone would be enough to win the day come day's end, but such a contingent might be sufficient to hold off the enemy long enough for Houston's army to reach us before an assault was launched in force.

Resolved to continue to dispatch couriers so long as they were dispatchable as I had dispatched so many already, I implored Fannin—who I knew for a brave man, if a supremely self-interested, often erratic one—to *move*, and with all expedition.

Could I count upon him, this Georgian cannoneer and self-confessed Houston myrmidon? The question was moot. I had no choice but to count upon him. I had to count upon him. Whether I counted upon him or not was wholly immaterial. He would march to our relief, or he would not march to our relief. He would arrive in time, or he would arrive too late, or he would arrive not at all.

He would. He would march. He would arrive in time. Because he must. Because he could not do otherwise. Because he could not forsake us. His brothers. His fellow Texians.

I had every confidence that he would do so.

Every confidence. For the moment.

Travis Diary, Feb. 29, 1836:

44 degrees. Blustery raw. Today marks week one of our besiegement. Earlier, S.A. reiterated his offer of surrender, the same he had proffered us on day one. I was much tempted to accept it. I have women (9) and children (10) here, all of them sequestered in the sacristy of the chapel. It would have been both imprudent and irresponsible of me not to have given it serious consideration. But in the end, I was obliged to decline, although this time I did think better of doing so with a cannon shot. For the moment, we must only sit still and rely upon help arriving as I remain confident it soon must. But it does not come easily to the men. To wait. For the storm to break. Nor, frankly, does it come easily to me. That is one art, forbearance, biding my time, that always has escaped me. Escape! I daresay that escape from this place is precisely what many of us dream of now, for in truth, we are not "defending" this Alamo. Here could be anywhere. It could be the moon. We sought a refuge. Some asylum. We sought a sanctuary, not a citadel. These walls were available, close at hand, and we availed ourselves of their availability, though that hand has since become a fist, one closing tighter by the day. I feel for the citizens of this neighborhood, these innocent townfolk, however poor and ignorant, so thoroughly infected with papist superstition, who, through no fault of their own, find themselves snared upon the horns of a dilemma not of their making. We are prey now to news that is non-news, no-news, to rumor, gossip, whisper, conjecture, hearsay and hunch and guess. As much as it must remain the surrounding enemy outside our walls that occupies our attention, there grows the

suspicion that another enemy encircles us within. This fatigue of boredom. The exhaustion of vigilance. The dread of irresolution and debility of hope. Not ennui, *inanition*. It is Time itself, the inclining press of its passage, that we would give anything to lose track of, for each day it seems that we persist less even as we perish more. Col. Bowie, poor soul, is worse and worsening. Gripped by fever dream, he no longer can lift his head from his cot. The doctor, Pollard, is at a loss to say what ails him. Something "typhoidol," is his considered diagnosis. Whatever it is, it is a horror to behold. The little that is left of the man is but a smear suppurating beneath quilts where he is melting inexorably to so much levigated mucilage. When I visited him, mere hours ago, he was racked by a most horrid, sawtoothed yowl—*yaarrrgggghhhhh!!*—before gurging up the words, "*¡Fuera! ¡Si bien todavía se puede!*" I ask myself why these words—"Get out! Get out while you still can!"—the words of a dying man half out of his mind with mortal fever, should so discommode me. Whatever the good doctor administers—ginger, bromine, creosote, nitrate of silver, tincture of iron, lead, camphor, quinine, turpentine, potassium, ammonia, aromatic sulfuric acid, dover's powder, licorice, whiskey and rye, May wine and milk, as well as, so he tells me, salix alba, eupatorium, pefoliatum and oleum terebinthine—each fail, in his words, "to so much as slow the downward spiral of his condition." This diminution of a strong man. His reduction to a loaf of human fester.

Travis Diary, March 1, 1836:

34 degrees. Hard rains, harder winds. Blue Norther, Blue Whistler, Blue Darter, Blew-tailed Norther. Burr cold. Weather regardless, as of this hour, reinforcements have arrived, 32 from Gonzales through the enemy's lines under cover of darkness to huzzahs all around. Thirty-two! 320 would not be enough, not by half. Are we to take this as a sign that more are on the way? Are the settlements at last awakened and arising? Are these paltry few but the vanguard of thousands more? Is Houston's army readying to march to our relief at last? Is Fannin en marche even now? These Gonzales men say they know of no others. Lieutenant Bonham still is out, Sam Maverick and Captain Seguin as well. Despite the appearance of these 32, or perhaps because of it, I sense a shift of mood, a conturbation of spirit. How, really, could it be otherways? Existing— *surviving*—like animals amidst such muck and rubble, penned animals, pent-up animals inside an enormous hog wallow bundled enclosed one upon the other day in day out all day all night day after day, skin is gotten under, nerves are gotten on, petty irritations build to boiling botherations and tempers flare, words are exchanged, fists fly. Every family has its issues. But how we stink! Our stench alone must give the enemy pause. Discipline, I seem to recall General Washington observing, is the soul of an army, in light of which I must only judge us soul-less—filthy, infragrant and soul-less. A surfeit of skunks. A chine of polecats. Doldrum + Fatigue + Dread is a recipe for nothing useful. Time has become our noose; we sense its knot tighten to the navel of our necks. The men are left with little to do but to imagine the worst, and what can be

imagined always is worse than what is in fact the case. Tired, hungry, dirty, bored, scared. We all are scared. We all wish we were someplace, anyplace else. Fear can be faced. Fear can be mastered and vanquished. Properly harnessed, fear can even mobilize, it can galvanize. Absent fear, after all, what would we be? Fearless? Only a stupid man, or a barking mad one, is fearless. But dread, dread is different. Dread is a drug and it seeps into and slows all it settles through with lassitude, hebetude, desuetude, with torpor. Wherever it lands, it narcotizes the soul, weevils its way into every warp and woof of every waking hour of every sleepless day. It is left to me, no other, to conjure an effective antidote. In this, Crockett's fiddling is not unhelpful, but Crockett's fiddling is, after all, just that—fiddling. *¡Basta ya!*

Travis Diary, March 2, 1836:

34 degrees. Clear. No wind. To endure this daily ascent of the sun. The slow, painfully slow arrival of first light, its sash of pink strapped brute taut against the bruise of purple. Merciless. To awake each morning flopped in sweat breathing mortuary air. Monstrous. The way we wait. Then wait some more. Keep waiting. Still wait. Are left to wait. Compelled. Powerless. To do else but wait. For some word. An indication. But no word comes. And no indication. No one comes and then no one comes again. Where are they? Where are they now? Who are they now? When are they now? God forgive me, but I no longer believe help is coming. I no longer believe that if it does come it will reach us in time. I no longer believe that we will be rescued. I believe that we have been abandoned. Forsaken. Sacrificed. DESPERO ERGO SUM. There is no deliverance, no salvation. There is but ruth, wroth and ruination. There is but extravasation and exudation. For God is not here. God is elsewhere. God is otherwise occupied. God is everywhere we are not. What is here, is Evil. It dwells here. Abides here. I have seen It. I see It each day from a distance astride Its prancing pale horse, Aguirre. I have watched Him in my field glass for no reason save that He exists. I harbor no personal animosity towards Him. I do not know Him. My enmity exists in the abstract, my animus on principle. I despise what He represents, the values He personifies. I damn His soul. We are in control of nothing, He is in control of everything. He inflicts, we forbear. We are at His mercy, He has no mercy. And still, we wait. Still, I continue to dispatch couriers. How many have there been now? Dozens. I have lost count. So many. In the

beginning was the Word? Ha! Couldn't prove it by me. And the danger, for clearly it is a danger, of pleading so often for rescue, is that I become, inevitably, the proverbial Boy Who Cried Wolf. I am not cut out for the part I have been assigned to play in this…calamity. I need to pull myself together, but my hands refuse to cooperate and my heart is not in it. And yet, I am left little choice but to act contrary to my nature. I refuse to dream the dream of victimhood, but it is difficult. When under the gun, with none who will listen, it is difficult, difficult not to believe that life is penance, little but that to which we are sentenced for having dared to live it, mired hip-deep in *Mictlan*. It is difficult not to God damn James Fannin, to God damn Sam Houston, and wherever God is, to God damn God.

Travis Diary, March 3, 1836:

40 degrees. Crisp. Calm. Clear. The sun slapping down, its spank in slabs and planks. Bonham is back! (As Seguin is not. Yet.) At mid-morning, in broad daylight, Lt. James Butler Bonham galloped miraculously untouched through the dumbstruck enemy's lines to deliver us word that there shall be <u>no</u> relief, <u>no</u> rescue, that Houston has commanded that we evacuate this place upon the instant, is apoplectic about our not having done so earlier. So then it is as I had feared. We are abandoned to manage our fate strictly upon our own. Well, if nothing else, we now know that we can cease hoping, praying, dreaming, and so set about the business of either bargaining for our lives, or selling them most dear. Bonham also deposited with me a single written communiqué that, while most welcome in one respect, is now bounden to have little practicable effect. It reads:

> My true friend, you cannot conceive of my anxiety. We have not the slightest news of your situation and are given over to a thousand conjectures and conjurings about you. We await another 300 here from all points and vow to lose no time in providing you assistance. For God's sake, Buck, hold out until we can succor you. Best wishes to all your people there and tell them to hold on firmly by their <u>WILLS</u> until we arrive. P.S. Write us very soon.

> —R. M. Williamson, Cmdt. Ranging Companies
> Gonzales, DeWitt's Colony

God bless Willie. But now, it is time at last to write Rebecca. I must, but do dread doing so. What say, after all, and how in god's name say it?

Estamos tan jodidos.

To Rebecca

Mi Corazón, Mi Enamoré, Mi Virtuosa,

It is late and I write in haste as the enemy encroaches on all sides here not 200 yards from where I sit writing at a loss to fill the page with all the poetry my soul contains.

My belief in our cause, Bec, remains unshaken, though in the drab light of recent events I sometimes wonder whether I should not rue the day I came to Texas. And yet, had I not, I would not have met you, known you, loved you. Whatever may happen, know that I am possessed of no regret. I am possessed only of gratitude. I feel smiled upon. Graced. Graced and chosen. I feel impossibly blessed.

I dream of you every night, have dreamt of you every night since coming here, large with the desire to return to you over all distances, past all divides, missing you unto extinction. But dreams, Bec, dreams are parlous things, parlous and delicate, as butterfly wings. Because they fade away, take fragile flight, in our pursuit of them as they alight, often as not, they are destroyed

It is said that savage events, *eventos salvajes*, steer their own course, dictate their own career, predict their own outcome. Certainly they proceed according to their own grim logic, which is that of men, their virulence, that violence which seeks always to sustain at all cost a life of its own. The earth orbits, the world spins, bad men and good cycle through of their own accord upon their <u>hungry</u> rounds fed by the blood spilled in the name of a <u>mortal</u> meaning each seeks and seldom finds.

Our war never ends. There are merely lulls and lapses, longuers and lassitudes.

I do not know whether some things are worth dying for. Such certainty eludes me. I know only that some of us believe it is necessary to do that which is required of us, required by what we are, who we are, why we are, believe we are.

I love you Rebecca, more than I knew possible or might have wished or hoped or dreamed. More, certainly, than I deserve. This love the size of the sky. Were life otherwise, were it possessed of a kernel of fairness, we would die enraptured. Die in one another's arms. Die infinitely. Instead, whether we shall see one another again now appears doubtful, however much I should never be so happy as to be shed of this wretched place and returned whence I better, for love's sake, belong. It is, for me, as once the Psalmist wrote, "My soul breaketh for longing of Thee."

What the devil am I doing here, Bec? Once, I knew. Or thought I did. I thought I was doing my duty. How foolish I was! How mistaken! Not to apprehend that my death was to be considered by certain people the admissible cost of pursuing their own ends. I daresay that I have had more than my fill of self-sacrifice. The charms of martyrdom hold no allure for me. I am badly used, and about that, I confess, I am furious. The fault may be mine, the blame belongs to others. May they choke on it.

My god! All the ways a man, saint or sinner, martyr or marplot, can misspend his life. It is difficult, so goddamn difficult, to get anything right. Say it, write it, do it, right. It is hard to do anything worth its doing. Though perhaps it is never too late to learn about love, or how to die for it, however unsung, breathing in the last of its sun. That radiance. In <u>beams</u>.

Perhaps, who knows, if we are fortunate beyond what we deserve, someday someone somewhere may remember that something happened here that may merit its well-remembering. Perhaps our ruin will to future times be as past days are to us. But there is no correcting it. Not now. It is too late. Too late, I fear, for everything.

The fugue of history always is far-off until the moment it assails us. And then—may I chance a Latinism?—then *contemptus mundi*. No, should it come to it, I would much prefer not to be installed in a niche in History. Indeed, at the moment, I can imagine nothing that would distress me more.

The regrettable truth, my love, is that should we fail to be massively relieved in the next day or two, I am resolved to do whatever I can, whatever may be necessary up to and including negotiating terms of our surrender, to avoid what otherwise must be a tragedy of unthinkable proportions.

So then, do not hope. Rather, pray. Pray for us, Becca.

What comprises a life well-lived? Is mine one? What finally does it amount to? Or perhaps amounting to misses the point. Still, what can be its purpose when it leads to the sacrifice of all that makes it worth its living? Blake says that the path of excess leads to the palace of wisdom. Blake was wise, but first one must survive.

It, all this, can only be a love story, is it not so? That at last, and precisely that. A love story gone wrong. All wrong. Grotesquely wrong. Love of Tejas. Love of you. Love, too much perhaps, of Self. The story of what one does for love and what one does not. What one is willing to do and what one is not. What one finds oneself doing because it must be done.

I would have much preferred not to live a skeleton's life, but we seldom are permitted to choose which bones we pick, least of all with ourselves. Every man would be a paladin, a Galahad, every man a Lancelot, his own story's hero. And yet, tempt fate as he may, storybook it away, no man wishes to die. But then, neither does he wish to fail to book passage upon the one ship, the voyage of which is possessed of the promise to endow his life with some scrap of higher meaning. Insofar as such meaning may exist.

But does it?

I am faced now with the inevitable eleventh-hour questions. Does the way one dies matter? Does choosing the time, place and manner of one's death confer upon that death a measure of meaning or worth or value that it otherwise would not possess? Is there a distinction to be drawn between a "good" death and some other kind? And if there is, how draw it? Who draws it? And why?

Perhaps these are the wrong questions. Perhaps the right ones, right one, the only one is, does love really become greater, better, truer, does it thrive best in the midst of calamity, as the world shuts down and time runs out? The heart softens, Bec, softens and swells—too late to stop now the wayward rainbow in my soul—even as the hide heals harder by half.

Here I am staring death in the face, doing my best to spit squarely in its eye, and suddenly nothing could be clearer than that dead is dead. Just that. Only that. That alone. Mere, mundane, meh. Just so.

Oh, I may try as I am able to console myself that my blood may water this land, marry with its soil, sift through, sink, soak in, settle here, stain deep its sands, become one with the flesh of this earth knowing that this is how and where my love will die, for the sake of something still unborn, stillborn. But I know better. I know better now. I know that I am bounden to lose my life, and soon, to what amounts to little more than a mindless blunder.

I know the truth. I know that it is all so much fiction. The truth/is fiction.

Out of sight, out of mind, out of luck, out of time. No help, no relief, no reinforcement, no rescue, no succor or salvation. Our being here is no exploit, no feat or emprise. It is an act of monumental miscalculation.

Live, Becca, I bade you. Take pains to live at all cost. Live, then love better still, without tears or sorrow, fears or regret.

Live without *saudade*. Love with **_duende_**.

Thinking of you

plunged   plush   in prayer
Beneath this mesh of moon
Lifted, lush, lunging long
down the open eye of your throat

Your loving, Will*

*(Seven years after her fiance's death at the Alamo, an uncommonly propertied Rebecca Cummings—she owned at the time over 8,000 acres, half-a-dozen slaves and 125 head of cattle—married a San Felipe-based attorney who had migrated from Claiborne, Alabama to Texas in 1838. David Young Portis, four years her senior, was to become a state senator, then a judge. The childless couple remained man and wife for 30 years until Rebecca's death in 1874 in San Angelo, and her subsequent burial in San Antonio's Odd Fellows Cemetery, roughly twelve blocks east of the spot where some three decades earlier William Barret Travis had lost his life.)

To David Ayres, Montville:

Please take care of my little boy. If the country be lost and I perish, he at least will have the knowledge that he is the son of a man who died fighting to win for him that country's freedom. It is not much, but it is all I have to give.

It is everything.*

*(Following his father's death, Charles Edward lived with both his Travis and Cato relatives back in Alabama, his mother and her second husband, Dr. Samuel Grandin Cloud, having died in the New Orleans yellow fever epidemic of 1848. Returning to Texas, he was in 1853 elected to and served a single term in the state legislature before a brief stint with the Texas Rangers led to his being commissioned a Captain of Cavalry in the U.S. Army, a rank he held for roughly a year before being court-martialed and cashiered for conduct unbecoming. Entering Baylor University Law School, he was admitted to the Texas Bar upon his graduation as a member of the class of 1859. A year later, at the age of 31, unmarried and childless, he died of consumption at Chappell Hill, Texas.)

Travis Diary, March 4, 1836:

44 degrees. Gusty raw. Savage dawn. Vile light. I have neither slept nor eaten in three days, find myself nodding off now and again only to jar awake with brute starts undreamed to half-life. All is pervigilium here; tension pours like tears pulsing wettened as wounds from every weeping wall. Every hour of every day it is three in the morning. Minutes feel like hours, hours days. Moments turtle *agotado*. Listless. I see the laxity in the mens' eyes, the banjaxing, the hollowed, dead, fixed blank stare, staring at nothing, staring at the something miles off that is not there. Save holes. Holes in time and non-time. Hole after hole. They would dive deep inside them, plunge through and disappear. So many, too many, verge upon derangement now. Sapped and jangled, fevered and belly-sick, flavid about the gills, forfeit to the occasional raving hallucination. The greatest events in human history occur while we sleep. I cannot sleep. Nuit blanche after nuit blanche. Is there a point of no return? A breaking point? A rubicon moment when a limit is reached beyond which the enemy becomes oneself as much as any other? When the only conceivable escape is toward the one place one dare not go? So how much longer now? Tonight? Tomorrow? Sooner? Later? Instanter? Difficult to consider that the prospect at hand is less that we are soon to be no more, than that we continue stupidly to persist in our belief that we once were anything else. Between what is lurking out there, biding its lethal time, that which is on its way, oncoming and unstoppable, and that which is in here, mired unalterably in place, already gone or going, the choice is clear enough: there is no choice worth its choosing.

No one sees time save in its monstrous passage across long walls. These crumbling, half-tumbled walls. This is how it ends in the face of those who would skin you alive clean to the bone, peel you back like the pulp of a plum, chin to shin, buttocks to brow. Where, god-left, god-shed, god-shunned as every jackal named Judas, the breeze bends like a branch, the sun siphons red to the rim of its rind, and the only certainty available, the only inevitability, is the unswerving punctuality of chance. Angel of mercy become angel of death. The descent of beasts, hellbound on all five sides.

Out of the garden
into the jaws,
welcome home—*Odium fati*—
to Golgotha.

Morning, noon, eventide too
the sky blood red
blood black
and blue.

The Line

I remember standing before the men, my men, this omnium gatherum in the churchyard, the chapelyard, bracketed by the high adobe wall of the *Convento* to the north, and the earthen-embedded timber pickets of the *Empalizada* to the south, vowing to myself to render what was about to happen as quick and painless as I might manage to make it.

Behind me loomed the 90-year-old chapel, its native limestone, 25-foot-high Tuscan-style, quattro-columned, elaborately gadrooned and archwayed façade, owing to the enemy's week-and-a-half of cannonade, now a much battered, ocher-and-isabelline-colored wreck. The four pedestaled figures of its wall-mounted plaster saints—Francis, Anthony, Bartholomew, Clare (or perhaps Dominic and Ferdinand; some dispute)—were pitted and pockmarked, spalled, spalted and grotesquely gouged. Anthony had lost the better part of his head, Clare been dashed to stumps below the knees.

Here of late, I had been going out of my way to scant it, the chapel. There was about the place the whiff of sulfur, clack of knucklebones, the clanking of heavy chains. Still, I had selected this spot in preference to others because anything framed by an arch intrinsically is picturesque, and, while I harbored no expectation that this crowd in particular was like to appreciate how aesthetically apropos was the setting, for what I had in mind, no single quality was more fitting—and, I was hoping, effective.

The air felt like sleet. My teeth buzzled like blo-flies as they often did when the air felt like sleet. Clearing my sleet-corroded throat, I tugged at the wheel-wide brim of my hat while my eyes *dartled* right to left, left to right and I paused to wonder whether this wasn't the most difficult moment of my life in a life fraught with difficult moments.

"Contrary to what you may have heard rumored with respect to the purpose of my gathering you here," I began, "I wish at once to make clear that I am disinclined to scratch, sketch, or otherwise draw a line in the sand with my sword. Not only"—I clutched my coatflaps, batwinging them wide to either side—"am I not wearing one, but if I were, such a gesture— cheap stunt, actually—not only would be gratuitously theatrical, but place each of you in the unpardonably impossible position of having publicly to declare your intention to leave or stay, a decision, a *choice*, that clearly is yours to make strictly in private, a sacred matter between you and your God."

The wind, I knew, was scattering my words like jackstraw; I suspected that for all those to the rearmost could hear, I might as well have been speaking in tongues. That said, those 250 men—despite their cud-chomping jaws, chins juiced brown, the cheeks apple-bulged with chaw—were more attentive than I had anticipated. Or, perhaps, after enduring a fortnight deprived of a decent night's shut-eye, they were asleep on their feet, dead to the world, a world that at present was arrayed hard against them in four directions as far as their eyes could see.

When one of the men bellowed, "Louder!", I squared my shoulders, tossing the sunbright colors of my *zarape* over my left, then hooked my thumbs into the accordion-pleated sateen of my waist sash. The wind was whippy; when it gusted, it backcurled the brim of my cream-colored Quaker crown hat like a scroll.

Swaying some in place, I bent slightly forward at the waist and leaned full-faced into the full-faced wind, my right leg firmly planted, my left somewhat less so, the knee of the latter canted, the hip of the former cocked, though not eccentrically; contrapposto. Coupled with the rakish angle at which I had corniced my hat, I cut, as I considered it, a rather Hogarthian figure, one not unillustrative of his classic, "Line of Beauty." And this only underscored and reinforced the performative, or theatrical, sense of the moment.

"What I wish to say, men," I said, raising my voice to its limit, "what you need to hear and digest, is that we are out, I mean *all* out of both time and hope. Can you hear me? In the back there? Yes? No? Louder still? All right.

"I need not tell you that the enemy presses nearer our walls each day, nor that no reinforcements shall be reaching us. We have been abandoned to suffer our fate on our own, the truth of which is that the enemy outnumbers us 30 to one and if we choose to remain here and resist, we shall be crushed. Doubt it not. Murdered to a manjack.

"It is the numbers, you see. Six-thousand of them, 200 of us, 250 of us. Words may lie, numbers, even those as imprecise as the ones available to us, do not. Our exact number does not matter. What matters is that that number is insufficient, laughably so."

Pacing back and forth, to and fro before them, I prayed that, as I did so, my stride might appear more surefooted than it felt.

"I have written my soul out. For the past fortnight, I have written plea after plea, appeal after appeal, jeremiad after cri de coeur. I have dispatched two dozen couriers to broadcast our plight pillar to post. But now, now my well is run dry, my quill is quit, and my words—there no longer can linger a question—have been ignored. They have failed to rouse our brethren. And about that"—I reined up then, full stop, swallowing hard around the risen fist in my throat—"I *am* sorry. More sorry than you can know. My words have failed you, as I have failed them."

A roundelay of muttering rippled through the assembled, until at some length a voice called out, "No siree, Colonel. You ain't failed nobody. You give her all you got. You give her yer all. You give her hell. No man coulda done her more or better. This fix here ain't yer fault."

This, I don't mind saying, moved me. I was genuinely moved. "Why....I....I thank you, soldier, but I cannot agree. As your commander, the fate of this place, as likewise the future of Texas, is my responsibility and no one else's. That is just the fact, one that merits neither qualification nor stinting.

"The situation, then, is this. That should you wish to leave, then now, tonight, may be your last, best opportunity to do so. No one doubts your grit, but pluckluck and spit gets you only so far. No one is going to think less of you should that be your decision. Wait until dark, and then"—I gestured to my left, toward the Palisade, that low stretch of earth-staken timber pales—"shag it up and over the walls and into the chaparral beyond.

"As our intelligence places 500 of the enemy's cavalry out there on patrol night and day, armed with their damn nine-foot-long *lanzas*, it serves no honest purpose to pretend that the odds of your escaping unharmed are not stacked highly in your favor, but I leave that calculation to you." I paused. "But please, gentlemen, I admonish you, do calculate carefully."

Though remaining planted to a man in place, I noticed that at this, many of them ducked their heads, clawed their scalps, bunched their shoulders, scuffled their toes, rubbed absently at their necks and midsections and houghed and spit some in the dust as they glanced nervously sidelong in silence each to the other. Nothing could have been clearer to me at that moment than that they were torn, afflicted with every manner of mixed emotion. And why not? They may for the most part have been hopelessly illiterate, but a flock of imbeciles would have reacted no differently.

"What you need to know," I continued, "is that no finger shall be lifted by any man here to impinge upon or impede any who might wish to roll their dice in that fashion, and *Vaya con dios, y mi bendición.*"

It was then that I found myself inexplicably imagining overhead the *zopilotes*, the buzzards that had yet to appear in anticipation of what they uncannily must already have sensed was the imminent end of us. In my mind's eye, they circled absent queedle or complaint, their eerie silence rendering them more menacing than had they gabbled like a clutch of scrummaging magpies. Theirs, I could not help thinking, could only be the premonitory patience of those creatures who wait upon the transpiration of calamity, scenting the rot of death upon the winds of the very air they travel.

"So then, as clear and as simple as I can make it. Stay and fight—and die. Run away—and die anyway. Or, *or*"—I paused a moment, prolonged moment, protracted moment, permitted the prospect of what I was about to say sufficiently to penetrate— "remain here and solicit the enemy for terms of our surrender."

I waited. Not a mutter, not a mumble, not a murmur.

"Know, men, that I do not undertake this decision lightly. I have pondered the matter at length, considerable, *patriotic* length, and while I do not know that the enemy will condescend to offer us such terms, much less honor them if he does, it may, there being no viable other, be an avenue worth further exploration.

"It is, all said, I grant you, a most forlorn and desperate measure, but my primary object, as it must be, is to save as many lives as possible. *Your* lives. To salvage what we can, strike a bargain that ensures some form of clemency short of our annihilation, and retire from this field with honor. Were I to do anything less, I would be derelict in my duty as your commander."

Still, to my surprise, nothing but silence.

"And so we arrive at the reason for my summoning you here. To alert you to my decision to propose to our enemy an honorable secession to these hostilities. Let us pray that he has the good sense to accept it, for if he does not, it is my intention to make him pay most dearly on account. Indeed, should it come to it, I promise you that we shall hurt him, wound him, bleed him so badly that the ashes of his victory will taste to him more bitter, more *pyrrhic*, than could any conceivable defeat."

It was quiet enough to hear what I took for the rush of the wind shredding the clouds to sawdust, when of a sudden, the familiar KA-BOOM!—distinctly louder these days owing to the enemy's cannon having over the past fortnight drawn that much nearer the walls—was followed by the no less familiar red-hot whiz, whoosh and whistle, the *siss* of a cannonball *whortling* high over our heads, before crashing harmlessly into the corral in the vicinity of the latrines along the East Wall.

"Ah," I ventured less matter-of-factly than bemusedly. "I do believe that they continue to gun for us. Potshots—or ought I say, potty." Then tried to smile.

"It is no secret," I continued, "that Santa Anna is possessed of all the scruples of a whoremonger. This is a creature who has the temerity to proclaim not only that, '*Hombre es nada; poder es todo*': **Man is nothing; power everything,** but that, '*So yo fuera Dios, me gustaria ser mas*': **If I were God, I would wish to be more.** They do not call him *El Carajote*, The Big Prick, for nothing."

As intended, this occasioned a wave of uneasy laughter, though it was quickly spent. "That we must rely upon such a man to honor our request, is most discouraging. Frankly, I would sooner woo a scorpion. But"—I shrugged—"when one finds oneself hived in hell, the only way out—there can be no other—is headfirst through the devil's own door."

> *Coming Through Slaughter*, I recited to them,
> *seldom is easy—*
> *it gets pitched*
> *where dear friends*
> *dare not*
> *follow*
>
> *dear friends*
> **let the future storm—**
> **it will eat its own**
> **soon enough.**

"So then boys, for now, let us back up on the walls. Ears cocked, eyes peeled, peckers hard, powder dry. Prayers, if you've a mind, always welcome. And remember, men, that everyone, no exceptions, lives a life of scars to some extent. No one's suffering is of a higher order than anyone else's. We all got raw ordeals.

"Meanwhile, *cosecha de la fuerza de la noche, busque refugio en la tormenta.* Harvest strength from the night, seek shelter in the storm. We soldier on."

Gazing past, past or through the glaze of my looking glass, I could not help but reflect that over the course of the past fortnight I miserably had failed to keep up appearances. I gradually was losing touch with my recollection of myself. As if a mirror like a poem might be something to hide in or pass through, transfigured.

> White of the page. Silver of the mirror.
> *How many doors will this man open*
> Realm of the image. Regime of mirage.
> *And stand with his skull against the light*

Could I reach him across the pane of such a space? Was that possible? Did I wish to? Peel off his image? Chip it with a chisel? (Letting him fall where he might, bent backward, slantwise, simulacrum reversed!) Pour my arm through its sheet of sheer silver, clutching what I could sleeved to mercury. Strain him nickeled out the tin of the tain to bathe him the recombitant color of star? Clean as chrome.

> There is little enough to make of any of this but the inevitable shatter. The way life fractures, falls apart before it occurs, its walls collapsed, full-measured with blood. When the mirror cracks and you trip, slit your neck open *snik!* deep-wide upon its shards, what difference then? The image bleeds no less surely than the man. Astonished, you stare, disbelieving. Blood stares back at you.

That makeshift masked man going through his mis-spent motions arranging his cravat in the mica of his mirror has left one duty only: to die, estranged, alone, holding back that which cannot be held. And, meantime, come the chemical dark of the cobalt moon, live another day closer to death.

Outpatient

With what I construed for the end now all too clearly in sight, we were running low on victuals. Down to bed of seed corn.

To the rear of the compound's hospital on the second floor of the *Convento* along the East Wall (then filled to overflowing with the sick and injured), was a low-walled backyard or corral, perhaps 100 by 200 feet, and it was there on the evening of March 4th, what I in any event took for March 4th, that I stumbled purely by hazard upon one of our men—name known, but in the moment, try as I might to haul it up, unavailable to me—shambling aimlessly barefoot and bare-arsed, makeshift hospital smock flappling in the breeze.

Approaching the poor fellow with the intention of gently reproaching him back to infirmary, as I sidled nearer stepping purposely around a cannonball-blasted, buzzard-ravaged beeve's head, I could see that the poor soul's eyes were peculiarly bright with fever—mooncalf-bright, I thought to myself—even as they sought and failed to find, darting this way, goggling that, barrel-rolling in their sockets.

It was not until I spoke up—"Now soldier, what have we here?"—that the wretch seemed at all aware of my presence. At the sound of my voice, he plunged to his knees, pawed at something in the dirt, scooped it up and raised it to his mouth before stuffing it inside, commencing wolfishly to chew, or rather, chomp, which is to say gum it, for as I was quick to discern, he had not a tooth left in his head. Indeed, the gums themselves, which were so swollen that they bulged beyond his lips, were intervaled with irregular gaps where the gingiva had sloughed away or broken off completely. In consequence, his lower jaw, the little of it left intact, required that it be cradled loosely in place by a ratty strip of oily rag slung beneath his chin, then drawn up, over and tied in a rabbity-eared looking bow atop his head.

Retrieving the item from him—it entailed no little struggle, weak as he was, to wrest it from his jaws—I noticed that it was a discarded, flaxseed, meal-and-lard oil, muslin poultice, what commonly was called a mush poultice of the sort typically used to treat boils, lesions and pustules. Its saturated underside was smeared pus-yellow and yolk-bloody.

"Give it back," the poor soul managed, jaws click-clacketting as he somehow wrestled himself wobbling to his feet.

His age I found impossible to peg. He might have been as young as myself, he likely was older by half. His flesh was jaundiced and the color of jaundice and he smelled more than slightly unpleasant.

"I mean to et that thar," he said. "I a-spied her first. That thar's mine by rights of first finder. You've no proper claim to her. You go and give her on back now. You give a man a meal. You show a man some mercy."

Each word was as the grinding of a gear, bone-on-bone gear.

"About that you are perfectly correct," I replied evenly. "I have no claim, nor do I desire one. But if I permit you to…..*et* it, you will be dead before morning, your death will not be pleasant, I will have been complicit in having hastened it, and that can and will not happen.

"Besides, I cannot spare you just now. I need you son. I need you to fight against those Mex. I need you with me to go against Santana."

He stared at me, a study in incredulity. "You don't unnerstan' nuthun, do ya? I'm a-dead where I stand. You hear't them lungs?" His chest was a coffin of croup. "Now you look me all up and down. This here's a dead man yer talkin' to, boy. You think I'm a-leavin' here alive? I got the shits too bad, my teeth is all falled out, my eyes is going fast, and the gang-green's got aholt too far down to stanch 'er on back."

Lifting the hem of his gown above his head, he exposed the flesh rot that had spread its bismuth-and-bitumen corrosion yoke-like along his shoulders, sludging all down his arms to his biceps. From the base of his neck to the tuck of his armpits he looked—"torched" was the word that occurred to me. Sphacelated. I tried not to look away.

"See? What'd I tell ya? Don't matter. Them Mex don't matter none to me." His hacking was rackled with bloody phlegm. "I'm a goner any whichaway. All that matters is I got me a powerful hunger"—he pointed to the poultice clutched in my hand—"and that thar's as right a meal I've had since can't say when. And iff'n it's my last"—he shrugged—"suits me. Cuz I've about had enough of this here nuthun', sonny boy. Had my fill. All a man can stand."

His rheumy eyes were a wound of pleading.

"Seen that dog?" he said suddenly glancing nervously about.

"Pardon?"

"That dog. Seen it anywheres? Run off, must of. Spooked it. You did."

"Dog?" We had none there, not a pooch; Bowie had not brought along the Basset. "Afraid not, son. No dog."

"It was here all right. I was set to et on it. Dogs is devil smart. Up and found hisself a hidey-hole, musta."

I knew neither where to go nor what to do with this. "What kind, could you say?"

"What's that?"

"The dog. Can you describe it?"

"Dog?"

"The one you say you saw."

"Why? You seen it?" He paused. "Say, you fixin' on ett'n that thar?"

"All right, son, all right. Here then." Handing back the poultice, I turned, and, without a backward glance, hastened off, resisting the impulse to wipe my hand down my pants leg.

I had no tears left, no sorrow, but I did have a hunch. I had a hunch that for some of us, it was not so easy being dead. I had a hunch that being dead was infinitely more difficult, a far more complicated affair for some than it was for others. And that this poor fellow, this forsaken soul, the one I had just as much as murdered, did not really exist. That he was a ghost. A shade. A wraithing. One that, come morning, I would have forgotten all about.

As would he.

Not a single suicide. Surprisingly. Not yet. Just madness. Rampant as wishes.

Emerging at noontide, I churned muck across the compound's courtyard spoked with men spooked and armed to their hilts before halting hubwise for a moment bareheaded in the rainblow to stare straight up at a sky reefed with clouds close as roofs and shake a fist at the facts that sharked there. Left-handed fist.

Pitched right into a world of wrong until the wrong is wrung, rifted, burled, contrary to nature. Your own as well, I thought, standing there staring straight up, rain siphoning off my face, maniac tongues down my neck licking inside my shirtfront.

I thought: a man could go mad leashed to certain facts, entangled in their net of amber.

Standing there soaked through as laundry in the isinglass rain, it occurred to me that I never had fared well in their company, facts. Fallen in line with, genuflected before, saluted the facts the world had handed me. Would have me have. Encumber me with. The ones amassed outside these walls. Their machinery of bone. Debrided bone.

Handed half a chance I knew they would wrestle sky to earth. Gnaw down the sun. Grind star to sand. I knew they would nail the world, wafer to a wall. Or blast it back to bedrock. Until there was nothing. Nothing left. Not even chalkdust. Just/fact.

I preferred my own. To wand them left-handed sphinxed from spindrift, or wholecloth riddled from floss.

Now, Santa Anna, He Mother-born to Give and Not Take Orders, was a man of fact. Donned them like cladding, armor, Saurian armor. Those of the world, the one he strode, the one he strutted, irreducible, irremediable, literal as carbon.

Facts hate, and handed half a chance will not hesitate to kill you, pursue you even beyond the grave. Uncoffin your corpse, drag it to hell, kick it in the teeth, hand you your head, hang you by your heels, meathooked leftfooted as the deadweight of God.

Facts are the enemy. Facts are soul-less. Facts are the Devil's façade.

Travis Diary, March 5, 1836:

68 degrees. Clear. I have dispatched Mrs. Juana Alsbury, the late Ursula Bowie's sister, who for the past week has so selflessly been vetting the suppurant, impossibly contagious Colonel Bowie, with our proposal of surrender to Santa Anna. I presently await her return with the reply which will determine our course henceforward. We are prepared, either way, to lay down our arms, or to die fighting wielding those arms to the last. Earlier, I encouraged those who wished to leave here to do so before it is too late. I am aware of but one of our number who so chose. In truth, there are moments when I wish I was that man. Oh, to be possessed of the freedom to hotfoot it on cloven hoof! Idle wish! The only question now is whether surrender will be enough to mollify our enemy. In truth, I suspect not. I suspect that he is intent upon our murder as a declaration of his policy of pogrom and extermination, that he proposes to use our deaths as an example, an object lesson, a bloody warning that he is prepared to lay waste to one and all. In this, his effort to intimidate and overawe, he badly miscalculates. While to their everlasting shame our friends and neighbors will not be stirred to succor us, I cannot think that our deaths will do else but rouse them, if not in the name of Texas, then in that of exacting a most violent and personal revenge. Santa Anna does not know them, the way they rile, the capacity of their spine, but he soon shall learn, and then hell to pay and no pitch hot. Meanwhile, the doctor, Pollard, informs me that he expects Colonel Bowie to moan his last upon the instant; there no longer exists a shred of hope for his recovery. Well, every war records its waste; perhaps

the only true measure of victory is how one lives on or fails to in the face of defeat. What is it that we most dread about death anyway? Is it not, perhaps, that once gone, once absented, we—and all that our lived lives once meant, to us if to no one else—shall be not only forgotten as if we never existed, but that insofar as we are remembered, we will be *gotten wrong*? Misconstrued. Behind our back. That the undertaker will part our hair on the wrong side while mis-spelling Travis, Travers? And no one remaining who gives a dry enough fuck to correct him. We all fear being plotted against after we have been planted. You die, are dead to the world, only to have that world remember you, immortalize, *in error*. A fabrication. Gross fiction. A lie. Death always is less final than forgetting.

Santa Anna

As is his wont on the eve of battle, Santa Anna, a.k.a. He Who Can Do Anything He Wants, is catnapping, so when Almonte jostles him awake by placing his hand upon, then gently squeezing his shoulder—which being the site of an old wound is as sensitive as a weathervane—*El General* makes little effort to disguise his annoyance.

"Owww, goddamn it! *¿Qué demonios es esto, eh Almonte? ¿Por qué perturbas mis sueños?* What the hell is this? Why do you trouble my dreams?"

"*Lo siento, mi General, pero* we are just now in receipt of a communiqué from the traitor Travis."

The illegitimate son of a parish priest, the 32-year-old, U.S.-educated Almonte is an erstwhile Mexican newspaper editor who has known Santa Anna for more than a decade. For the past two weeks they have shared a single-story, limestone house (lent gratis for the purpose by its owner, Manuel Yturri y Castillo) tucked neatly into the northwest corner of *Bejar's Plaza de Islas* in the middle of town.

"*Por qué?*" says the Napoleon of the West flinging aside with a theatrical *swish* a silk sheet the color of new butter to reveal a brocaded, below-the-knee nightshirt the color of mint jelly. (His kincob one, to which he decidedly is more partial, is being laundered.) Swiveling on his non-extant butt, he swings his deeply scarred legs over the side of the bed in advance of placing his silk-stockinged feet, size 7 ¼, flat upon the terra cotta floor.

The room smells diffidently of having lately been fumigated with an incense of white copal (*copaifera officinalis*), a distinctive scent featuring subtle hints of rainforest woodiness, sunbright citrus, and a spicy, creamy balsamic less peaty than peppery. Reputed to cleanse the spirit, clear the mind, calm anxiety, stimulate creativity and awaken the deepest stratas of the soul, the fragrance is one that Almonte finds singularly cloying.

"Excellency?"

"I said *why*. Why Almonte? Why would you believe that anything a creature of that sort, *un bandido, una pirata, un forajido, un vagamundo*, might have to say would interest me in the slightest?"

"Ordinarily, *mi General*, nothing would lead me to believe *una cosa tan ridícula*, such a ridiculous thing. However, *en este caso*, in this instance, might I respectfully suggest that you...."

Sensing impudence, or mockery, Santa Anna barks, "No, Almonte! I will not waste my time, *mi tiempo*, which you of all people know is precious, *más preciosa*, upon such, such..... pointlessness! I have no wish to read it, not a word!

"We muster at midnight, attack before dawn. They lose, we win. They die, we live. Nothing can change that now, least of all some meaningless *palabras* penned by some *bandito Yanqui* who magnanimously was handed the opportunity to surrender to us—how many days has it been now?"

"*Doce, mi General.*"

"Twelve! Twelve days past! And who not only refused to do so, but answered us—*¡piense en ello!* think of it!—with the consputation of a cannon shot. I am not a merciless man, Almonte, as you of all people are aware, but my compassion, *mi compasion*, has its certain limits. Dare exceed them, as this Travers creature has so dared, and as you likewise are aware, there must follow certain consequences, *cierto consecuencias*."

"I understand, Excellency. *Por supuesto*. Of course. As you wish. But if I might take a moment, *con su permiso*, to read just the most pertinent passage...."

"Pertinent? Really? Pertinent, Almonte? Surely you can only mean **impertinent**."

"Ha! *Si. Por supuesto, mi General*. Impertinent. *Esta bien.* Very good."

There ensues a pause, one that does not so much linger as dangle in mid-air, during which Santa Anna looks expectantly at Almonte, and Almonte looks wonderingly at Santa Anna.

"So?"

"Excellency?"

"So, continue." A hand waved in impatience. "Proceed. Read your impertinent passage."

Almonte suppresses his smile. "As you wish." He reads. Finishes reading. Lowers the paper to his side having finished reading. The President of Mexico, he notices, is seated on the lip of the bed, eyes closed, evidently bored to unshed tears. "They offer to surrender to us. How do you wish to respond?"

When Santa Anna at some length slowly opens his eyes— they strike Almonte as they often have struck him, dark as suns, bright as shadows—what he sees there is something he has seen many times before. Less incredulity than disgust, less disgust than contempt, less contempt than unmitigated aggression, they glower with it.

"I do not," he says. "I do not wish to respond. I will not respond. There shall be no response."

"Very well, *my General, pero*, Excellency, such a courtesy, *una cortesía*, that is to say, protocol requires...."

Rising to his feet, Santa Anna shuffles to the window that opens onto *La Plaza* and its 100-year-old Cathedral of San Fernando, *La Iglesia de Nuestra Señora de la Candelaria y Guadalupe*. Save for a clutch of hobbled horses and a handful of low cook fires over which some few of his personal *escolta*, his presidential guard, *La Guardia Dorados*, can be barely delineated roasting ears of field corn, the plaza, redolent of horse dung and *habanero*, appears deserted. Following a moment of purposefully active silence, he invites Almonte to join him.

"There," he says pointing to the church. "What do you see Almonte? What do you see flying from the bell tower, just there?"

"I cannot see anything, *mi General. La oscuridad.* The darkness. It is too dark to see."

"*¿En serio?* Really? Then permit me to tell you what I see. I see a flag. A red flag. *Una bandera roja.* A red silk flag signifying no quarter, no mercy, no prisoners. A blood-red flag announcing that every one of the enemy, every **last** one, *cada último,* shall be put to the sword. That is my response, *Señor.* That is the only response such *chacales,* such *roedores,* such *gusanos,* such jackals and vermin and worms deserve, and I expect that response to be delivered this very morning at the point of sword, of saber, of lance and of bayonet, that *estos escorpiones,* these scorpions may not be permitted to grow! *¿Claro? ¿Soy entendido?* Am I understood?"

"*Perfectamente, mi General.*"

A gleam or gleaming enters Santa Anna's eye or eyes.

"I leave you with this, Almonte, and it is the last that I shall say upon the subject until victory is ours. If a man aspire to greatness, he needs, as the occasion may arise, to hold himself aloof enough from his own life to be capable of behavior that lesser men may judge not only morally reprehensible, but a sin against both God and nature.

"Let History record what I did here, not what our enemy said here. It is the actions of men, not their words, not their sentiments, not their sentences, their sentences least of all, that matter."

Can't say it better myself, and so will not try.

> It would take an endless length of time
> to describe the events of such a day properly,
> **in some inconceivably complex form** recording
> who had perished....and exactly where and how,
> or simply saying what the battlefield was like....
> with the screams and groans of the wounded and
> dying. In the end all anyone could ever do was
> sum up the unknown factors in the ridiculous
> phrase, "The fortunes of battle swayed this way
> and that," or some similarly feeble and useless
> cliché. All of us, even when we think we have
> noted every tiny detail, resort to set pieces which
> have already been staged often enough by others.
> We try to reproduce the reality, but the harder
> we try, the more we find the pictures that make
> up the stock-in-trade of the spectacle of history
> forcing themselves upon us....Our concern with
> history....is a concern with preformed images
> already imprinted on our brains, images at which
> we keep staring while the truth lies elsewhere,
> away from it all, somewhere as yet undiscovered.
>
> —W.G. Sebald

So the truth lay *elsewhere*, did it? Ah yes, now I remember, *away* from it all, somewhere as yet *un*discovered, or, perhaps, but recently discovered *in some inconceivably complex form* squirreled deep inside a steamer trunk—or was it a wine cask or butter churn or cider press or the leaves of a bible—stored in the loft of a log house—or was it a cowshed or corncrib or dovecot—raised originally by "Black" Adam Zumwalt in the Lavaca River region some 100 miles east of *Bejar*. The same, so some later would swear, whence Wee Jock Warnell—23 years old, five foot tall in his bootheels, 110 pounds soaked through, the sole Texian defender to have survived the massacre—had managed miraculously to escape. And where, despite what three months later would prove his mortal head wound, he strove in his few lucid, if trauma-confabulated moments, less to recount or chronicle, than to convey *in some inconceivably complex form* his idiosyncratic, if semi-coherent, not entirely indecipherable sense of the horror he personally had experienced:

To the Burrow's walls in the dark across difficult terrain race men clad in many colors going that extra mile because:
CHRIST'S BLOOD AND HEART ARE HERE....
splashes of red chaos
out of a jungle

"driven to the wall you'd put claws to your toes and make a ladder"
"Against this Wall, the way Brothers tear at/one another's Heads"

I

In the chapel the incoming oncome having clambered,
climbed, scaled
the permeable membrane

landsliding through the funnel of the ornamental gateway
  (no campanulate)
   where men and guns/with guns
rally to the entablatured escarpments to enact the
pro forma tragedy until

O! O no!

The Colonel! The Colonel is down!

Watch how he dies now, our Colonel, young Colonel,

how the brave young Travis dies

"DUENDE" (he whispers)

II

all that currently is the current case =
Outcome of the Historical Dynamic
unfortified by   war, namely:

heads on pikes
hides on frames
eyes on skewers
hearts on hooks
peckers on racks

the going price of any orthodoxy

ramified by what's at stake arcing along
untrackable trajectories   far   afield

per the PHYSICAL problem in kinetic principle

III

A cathedral
armor-cladded (fragmentary construction decorated/
desecrated for Christ)

90 years ago arose   impaled   upon a bayonet of faith

a mission imparting muffled messages to its natives: salvation
sin
survival
self-im-mo-lation

throughout this dead earth   —SHADOWLANDIA—
upon its sterile ground   previously dormant
recently roused

fluctuating through

penances & absolutions & the many fine madnesses
of prayer

IV

before the military charged in
(the Flying Company; *la Compania de Vuelo*)

the priests were chased out   chanting war songs   remote in time

Jesus was surrounded then   by soldiers
their lust their guns their dice their mezcal
sacramental wine drunk warm as warm rain,
smoother than silence

stonemason walls howling with coarse laughter
whilst Christ's blood dangled from the ceiling
and by torchlight unparalleled violence
ensued selectively indiscriminate

the next scene is:

V

hipwading endlessly   through red mist red mist red mist
muttering, evolve or revolt: "Are other choices
soon to be made available?"

the edifice over-stormed, battered to mineral   the sudden
falls
of adobe walls

whilst tapestries are slashed/
   crosses knocked slaunchways/
      stained glass shattered/
         censers and thuribles sent clattering/
            altars and installations, *retablos y laminas*
              overturned and strewn/
                  vestments violated (stained scarlet & torn)

ejecting colonists by hand-force   without possibility of egress
expulsionists and eradicators   killing with abandon
                      without expression
while I hipwade endlessly through redmist watching:

Bowie die brainsplattered upon his cot
Bonham fall disemboweled across chapel-high walls
Crockett? whereabouts unknown (evermore)

culminating (inevitably, predictably)   in
        trundled corpses bundled on tumbrils
        stacked ripe to the rafters   white-powder memory
                      exploding sky-high
                      denting the sky
                (because the sky's/the limit)
with the ashen floes of their souls

VI

                the dead   dashed
bashed in   trampled on   crumpled   sapless and shrunken
grown ancient while
        hacking their way, calvarium-free   to God
           toward (waiting) oblivion, obliteration
               and the gallows (waiting)
               uncosmic, chaosmic
                  beyond

```
c HA(!) os
r
e
A-cosmos     m
T        f      i
E               g
s LAUGHTER
                A
             pasT
                i
          preSENT
                gO(!)
                W
                A
        fu-tu  Re
                d
```

Death always is on time. Indeed,

**In all those stories the hero
      is beyond himself into the next
      thing….**
                       going into death.

One moment I was striding to and fro atop a wall—not just any wall, the North Wall—still half-asleep beneath a suffering saffron sky. The next I was shot in the head, skull shattering above the brow, musketball a blowdart through my brain as I lurched grotesquely, a window-stunned bird, in advance of pitching slack-jawed to my knees, slowly dying, dying slowly, if with a startling paucity of bloodfuss.

The good news is that I do not know I am dying because, being brainshot, I am cognitively incapable of accessing such knowledge.

The bad news is that I am dying anyway.

Typically, the last thing "the young" think about is death, but death was everywhere that day. It was unavoidable. I saw it. It stared me, teeth-bared, in the face. Even in the dark, I could not take my eyes off it.

On the other hand, death, being death, could have cared less whether I or anyone else was thinking about it. When death comes, it comes as it will, as it wishes, regardless. When death arrives, it does so indifferently, warranted or otherwise, with or without permission.

Death is possessed of its own momentum, as, too, its own valence and volition, as also its own endless *ennui*. No stopping it. No slowing it up. No deflecting or negotiating. No deals to be arranged, bargains struck, petitions or eleventh-hour appeals. Young, old, fair, middlin', death neither discriminates nor recognizes distinctions. It does not need to, and wouldn't, one suspects, in any case. Death, the ubiquitous leveler, always wields the upper hand, and what that hand wields, is weaponized.

Death is not interested in knowing your name. William Barret Travis meant nothing to it. It is not that discerning. It does not concern itself with your strength of heart, or staunchness of nerve, or eloquence of ink-dipped quill.

That day Death unlaced the sutures of history and fed ravening upon its wounds. It existed only to ensure that life wrecked itself, and if you happened to be William Barret Travis, and you found yourself where you found yourself, that time, that place, it wrecked it not a moment too soon.

ON A WALL, A WONDERMENT

And "*now let us talk of slaughter and the slain.*" Let us talk now about what happens when the end, the endless end, keeps ending over and over again. Because I was wondering. Is it true that you lingered there lockjawed and lobotomized, knocked pivot-wise blind as braille, tottering about like a Hottentot, your shellshot *cabeza* leaking memory of all you once were, no longer are, never will be again?

Let us talk about how no crusade crusades absent its cost. How zealotry is pricey, pays poorly for the forfeiture made, the body count, KIA's. How a second behind or a second ahead, turn right instead of left, and all of history implodes.

Let us talk about how anyone, yourself for instance, can valorize himself out of existence, sacrifice all in the name of what's right. How any dolt can die in his prime facing the music of *El Deguello*. Because being brave never bought a brave man a moment more or less. Because courage? That kind of courage comes carapaced in coffins.

Let us talk about how nothing lasts, whether mission or fortress—how fossilize fear?—prison or charnel house—frame gore in a mirror?—outpost, citadel, indefensible lair, how nothing is enshrined frozen in time, not even history's hoofprints....

> *"It is easier to raise a shrine*
> *than bring the deity down to haunt it."*

....save nothing, the nothing more that breeds more nothing, each life post-mortem the moment it's lived, waiting for the end mothed in the silence of smoke thicker than heat and as tall. (And you thought, how quaint, that there was less than an infinitude of ways to butcher the world or embolden its madness, simply by wielding words like weapons powerless as any poetry?)

Let us talk about how your own death dazzles me. All these years later. Still does. And how it keeps on dying, posthumously gasping for air in those pockets trapped between dream and deed. Nothing like one's last breath—eh?—to rouse one's second wind, year after year after book after book after page after page of superfluous words wrung dry of their drama, leaving what passes for a present, pyrrhic in its passing, the past your public pants for. While you, aghast at their applause, can only recall how much of everything must be forgotten, to remember anything at all.

> *"History is the splitting of heads*
> *to powder....We mutilate*
> *and call it wisdom."*

Let us talk about what any of us wouldn't give for a little well-earned obscurity. To be granted quittance enough to go unrecognized. Inside an occluding shadow, perhaps, or plunged down some pitfall gray as monotony and thinner than ellipsis above the fray, beyond harm's way, where what matters ceases to matter, and the adulators hold no sway, content to do one's anonymous time by hourly killing it.

I have a question for you (you need not answer it): Is it the dead who walk with the living, or the living who wander the dead? (Should not what is buried stay buried?) And you? Where are you? Hmm? Hiding? Hidden indelibly immune to transcursion, illegibly far-flung beyond your furthest inscrutable framing? As when fabrication extracts fact, the syntax of which nightly shifts in what room, upon what shelf, inside what urn, its ashes strewn between the pages of what book, sifting through the lyric of what tune.

Let us talk about your leaving some remnant behind. A heartstring, perhaps, a fallen tear or rueful gaze cast back to the callow youth you once forsook to pilgrim out armor-clad and chivalrously cursed, in thrall to a calling archaic, apocryphal, to a fate as self-created as self-coerced, one gantlet-run through the worst of all worlds.

Let us talk about memorializing a hero manqué whose feats were made of clay, and the way lies become legends and legends survive; the way myths multiply mystifies me. You? Too?

> *"You have to remember the past rather*
> *clearly if you are going to lie your way*
> *out of its existence, but you also have*
> *to be able to enter your new history so*
> *completely that it replaces the truth*
> *even in your own mind."*

I have another question for you (and expect an answer): Why is it always the worst that gets reprised? The wars we most remember? The massacres that wound the worst? Why all that joyless wickedness we most rehearse? Because, confess, that was just bad medicine, *muy mal*, all around. Tejas the body sickened, and you the surgeon assigned to saw her stem to stub, carve a collop of her corpus, some gyre of ground, a plat of plot to carry off deployed to free the amputee though it kill her stump by lopped-off stump.

Let us talk about how Man is thirsty and Life is drought. About how there is no asylum inside, no amnesty without. About how you made your life, and now must lie in it. Your death, and now must live with it, absent doubt. Not for a cause; hell, fuck the cause. But because you don't have to believe in death, to die.

"It is difficult at times to repress the thought that history is about as instructive as an abattoir."

(There should be one spectacular of ruin, red, mid-tragedy.)
for
(Often falling stars describe the incoherent…
While life bashes us thank God with colors.)

One moment I was asleep on my cot in my quarters midpoint along the West Wall half-dead to the world, the next I was jarred half-awake still on my cot in my West Wall quarters immersed in pitch-darkness. Jolted roughly half-awake on my cot in the dark in my quarters by a noise, an uncommonly loud if still distant noise or fugue of noises, a *tantrum* of noises the exact nature of which, because I was not yet fully awake, still sleep-muddled, left me befuddled and disoriented, feeling held oddly at arm's length while somehow melting against myself. This certain…remoteness.

But only for a moment. Because in the next moment, or perhaps in the moments immediately following, the succeeding next few, as I began in starts and fits to collect my wits, gather my bearings and find my firmer footing, as my head cleared and eyes focused and I swung fully dressed from my cot, rank, ripe, and radish-eyed onto my heel-worn, booted feet, it quickly became apparent that the noise, or, rather, the meaning of the noise—for it remained to me a diffuse if volumizing, rataplanned **drumble** despite my distinctly hearing a fair lot of banshee-style shrieking as well as successive round upon round of whoosheting and whistling—the meaning of the noise was that, as I exclaimed aloud, "Fuck! *¡Cono!* We must be under attack!"

¡La hora de la hora esta aqui!

Why, who knows, but as I yawned *en seriatum*, my mother's words came to me sudden as a gunshot. I heard her voice, if not her syntax, her voice, my syntax, a bark of clarity inside my head: "Pay attention to everything, William. Pay attention to each element of any situation. Isolate each element in high relief.

Examine each element from a variety of angles letting the truth emerge moment to moment upon its own unbidden slant."

My shotgun, Nock gun, the Hellblaster, leaned loaded against the wall at the head of the cot. Fetching it up, I called to Joe. Or tried to, for the words stuck, frog. I had to clear my throat before calling again for him to follow me out the door, "and bring the back-up," my Jaeger double-barrel *carabina*.

Frankly, I half-expected him to hang back. It was lost on neither of us, after all, that those bent upon <u>my</u> murder were citizens of a nation the constitution of which guaranteed Joe <u>his</u> freedom. If I had been Joe—well, I do not know what I would have done if I were Joe. I imagine I would have been mightily miffed, sorely conflicted, all the more so as our own just then published provisional Texas constitution contained the passages, not a word of which Joe, of course, was capable of reading:

> All persons of color who were slaves for life previous to their emigration to Texas, and who are now held in bondage, shall remain in the like state of servitude.

> Congress shall pass no laws to prohibit emigrants from bringing their slaves into the republic with them; nor shall Congress have power to emancipate slaves; nor shall any slaveholder be allowed to emancipate his or her slaves; nor shall any free person of African descent be permitted to reside in the republic.

As in the dark I shagtailed the 75 yards across the courtyard to the North Wall—I could not, I suddenly realized, feel my sleep-fruzzled feet; null set—I noticed that Joe, God bless him, God bless that boy, unhesitatingly, even eagerly was hard upon my heels.

And that the sky was scarred with fire, scabbed with fire. That the sky was arc-streaked with the horsetailed contrails of what I took for Congreve rocket fire.

I no longer recall mounting the 51-foot ramp to the loft-up of the North Wall. I must have, because the next I knew, I was atop the North Wall loft-up. Nor do I recall any Mexican bugles blaring the hair-raising fanfaronade of *El Deguello*, the ancient Moorish battle tune known as, "The Throat-slitting." Nor any Mexican war cries, whether that of, "*¡Vive Santa Anna mi dios de la guerra y justicia!*" or "*¡Los gringos son hijos de putas!*" or "*¡Muerte a los diaglos Tejanos!*" Hell, I do not even recall myself shouting as I ran, although it is said that that is what I did, "Come on, boys! To your stations! The Mex are upon us and we must only give them hell! *¡No rendirse, muchachos!*"

What I do remember remembering while standing up there, up on the loft-up, was the sense of being suspended 1,000 feet in the air amidst some ambit of cataclysm while our own cannon, those to either side of me, up-belched, out-roared and disgorged from the mouths of their muzzles the pro forma fan of superheated langrage—this sprayed, hotshot stew of scrap metal, stray shotting, horseshoes, nails, chainlink, belt buckles, pocket watches, door hinges, crumpled pots and pans, shard of metal kettle, what-all and what-not. I also remember how, despite the convulsive, concussive, utterly deafening detonative discharges, how dead quiet everything was. I might have been a million miles away.

I have heard it said that the silence of God *is* God. So, then, perhaps it was a blessing that I recollect so little, or the little that I do, so vaguely, indistinctly, with such a blurred paucity of detail. Strange, the wonderments available to those who seek the certain higher places, or, being sought, avail themselves thereof inside the summitry of the sky. But then, I was too busy at the time for such lofty thoughts, busy craning my neck and canting at the waist and, upon chancing a quick peek down over the wall, discerning through the darkness little but a swarm of movement bottlenecked at its base, this churn of humanity hived to a single, undifferentiated mass hurling itself, so my impression, like a battering ram against the wall's bulkhead while groping for such handholds and footholds and toeholds as might be afforded by the denticulated timbering of its reticulated façade.

It was a sight that, while I cannot account for the impulse even now, prompted in me the profound desire to drop trou and unleash upon their prettily beplumed and hatted heads, their resplendent gherkin green, pom-pommed, impossibly shiny black leather shakos, a lantrifying hot-arcing torrent of steaming micturation. A piss, as it were, into the Abyss. Which, after considering it for a moment, purely delightful moment, what I so wished to do, I to my eternal regret mustered the wherewithal to resist doing.

Men all along the loft-up were bellowing curses and imprecations even as they were being shot at and/or down, the latter falling backwards or pitching forwards or reeling sidewise before plunging from the platform to the ground below, more than a few pissing and beshatting themselves as they did so. Still others were hemorrhaging from their cranial vaults, or exsanguinating unto hypovolemia in dehiscent outstrewings, while the few who remained alive continued to heap their charred hands with improvised metal stuffing to load and reload the cannon in order to cannonade again and some more and some more again.

I smelled burnt flesh. Lacerated and burst intestine. Ate smoke, tasted blood, spat shit, or swallowed it.

Fingers were clipped off. Hands were cleaved off. Arms and legs were clopped off.

Faces and partial faces were blown clean away. Remnants of jawbone and face pulp, tongues and teeth hurtled this way and that in salmon-tinged flurries. Flesh and fatty bits of mesentery and omentum flumed the air like fumes. A segment of windpipe and chunk of calvarium whapped me flush across my left zygoma. Followed by, I might have sworn, a cremaster.

I heard myself scream at myself. "Run! What are you waiting for?" And again, "They have ladders, *scaling* ladders! They have crowbars and pickaxes and sledgehammers and their bayonets are three feet long!"

But I did not run. I could not run. I could have run, but I did not run. Because that was not my role here. That was not the part I had been bequeathed to play, the part I was assigned, which was to be dauntless and redoubtable and do what I was supposed to do: face the cut-throat music, look death square in the eye and refuse to blink, grit my teeth, smile awhile and stand my ground, to die self-sacrificed first to the foremost, or refrain from same as long as one of my men yet remained alive.

I glanced around, around the loft-up, left, right, front, back. My God! Where was everyone?

Where were Wash Cottle and Wash Main? Where were Will Wills, Free Day and Man Shied? Sixteen-year-old Gal Fuqua, where was he? Tap Holland, Gee Pagan, and Dolph Floyd, Tug Daggert and old Gumball Perkins, where were they? And where was Chas Zanco of Randers, Denmark, who had traveled farther than any of us here to have his hopes scotched and dreams dashed?

Joe, God bless him, was there, but everyone else was not there. Everyone else was gone. Had gone. Vanished. Up and disappeared. Or was dead. Or dying. I was there and Joe was there and no one else was there. No one who remained alive.

I see myself leaning far out over the wall, daredeviling its edge, acrobatically straining as far as I could, half-hanging there trapezed by my knees—no net, harness, no dry runs. I see myself aiming the seven brazed barrels of the Nock gun directly downwards at the writhing mass of manhood at its base and squeezing the trig ...

... up from out of the maelstrom below, propulsed by way of an India pattern Brown Bess British surplus musket at 600 to 1,000 feet per second, a .35 caliber buckball sucked the very eyes out of the air before it crashed into my cranium lifting me off my feet and spinning me clean around as it punched a divot in my forehead just large enough to accommodate a quilltip.

The shot could only have been one in a million, the outcome of cockeyed blind chance, the longest of long shots. Not that it mattered. Indeed, nothing could have mattered less, for even after all these years, it remains in every detail exactly the same: all predictable, all inevitable, all as wrong as wrong could be or ever was. (Before I so much as hit the ground, the rumors had begun. Even as I sensed my sphincter unpuckering, the rumors were gaining traction with friend, foe and stranger alike. That I had taken my own life. That the wound was too clean, too dead-centered, too neatly configured and tidily arranged, as if by design too purposefully, premeditatively singular to be the handiwork of other than that perpetrated by my own hand.)

Knee-buckled, I sagged, almost went down, staggered one, two, three steps before pitching forward and collapsing against the barrel of one of the cannon in advance of sliding slowly to the ground clawing the empty air, pawing the planked deck, laboring to haul myself to a sitting posture while notching my spine against the cannon's wheel.

I felt my hands convulse to doorknobs; subsultus. Felt myself dying *on cue*. Labored, even as they insisted upon closing, to keep my eyes open, as for the last time, they closed.

Can I say now what they saw then? At that moment?

I can try.

I can say that at last I saw that the dead are not like everyone else, that it was as if someone not alive was speaking: "Relax. What must be borne is only the unbearable, what suffered only the insufferable. Steady as you go. You're going. You're gone."

I can say that my eyes saw me dying in the dark at dawn, dying dingily, in obscurity, forsaken by my fellow countrymen, sacrificed not upon an altar, but a tumbledown dumpsite in the middle of a moon-cratered slag field engulfed by pitchblende darkness, while from North Wall to South, East Wall to West, an uncadenced carnage of over-determined cruelty ripsawed a mile a minute through every quoin and corner, cousy and crawlspace of that three-acre compound until everyone was dead at once, every last one, and I was left alone no longer gasping for breath in the gunpowder smoke and atomized bloodmist and attar of inside-out intestine in the atavistic dark of a reddened meatyard of human strewage, a sargasso of blood, lymph, chyle and chime, synovia, serousium and fluids peritoneal and cerebrospinal to tumble toward something so deplenished that no throb or pulse, flicker or twitch persisted.

I can say that, and I can say that there was no radiance. That there was a singular absence of radiance. Or should you wish, call it splendor. There was none of that. Or glory. No radiance, no splendor, no glory. Only a presence, the emanating, enveloping, overwhelming presence of all that is the opposite of radiance and splendor and glory.

And grace.

What did I see? I saw the skull beneath my skin. Shot through. Shattered. Bone-blasted. The end of thought; debris. A tousled dark, its darkness wet as rain. As any sea.

I saw the end of me:

Souring alongside the sun.
|
|
|

This conglomerate stillness

So now, if you will, pause a moment.
Consider and reflect.
Ponder it well.
Contemplate awhile.
Think/hard.

Is there anything in this world more *rending*
than the sounds of human slaughter
uncoupled from words?

And then, *likethat*, of a sudden
everywhere
all-at-once
the sound of stopped
breathing,
throughout a vast space
a resonant silence more silent than
$$\text{the silence of stars.}$$

He is dead then. The young man is dead. And so, being dead, is spared the affront of the Mexican *soldados*—themselves young, most of them, young as himself, younger than himself—who blunder up and pour over the North Wall and then over the other walls and spill into and overspread the compound and rout and kill everyone, butcher his entire command letting enough blood to slosh in, save the 62 or 66, roughly a quarter of the whole who scramble and phutscutter outside to the south and east and to a man are ridden down and through, transpierced by the mounted regiment deployed there for the purpose of preventing anyone from escaping murder by their nine-foot-long, straight-grained, beechwood-shaft cavalry lances fitted with their new and improved 10-inch-long, saber-sharp, forged steel, diamond-shaped, grooved-and-whelked, rabbeted impaling heads

∧ ∧ ∧ ∧ ∧ ∧ ∧ ∧

(advertised as killing "bigger, better, faster") that when withdrawn from back or belly, neck or eye, chest or ribs or groin, come away custardy and creamed with human gore.

Pigsticking. It ends, this *La Hora de la Verdad*, this *La Hora del Último Suspiro*, this matador fantasy, as it must, predictably, in so much presumptive pigsticking.

Point for them the virtue of slaughter,
Make plain to them the excellence of killing
And a field where a thousand corpses lie.

—Stephen Crane, *War is Kind*

Thirty, 40, at most 45 minutes later, it was all over, and Santa Anna was lounging in his tent, shrugging as he remarked to Almonte, "*Todo en un día de trabajo. ¿Un asunto de pequeña, es cierto, pero una victoria es una victoria, no? Ahora, es hora de sacar la basura. Los quemamos, estos....descartes. Todas los doscientos cincuenta y siete. ¿Es doscientos cincuenta y siete, no?* All in a day's work. A small affair, granted, but a victory is a victory, no? Now, time to take out the garbage. We burn them, these.... discards. All 257. It is 257, isn't it?"

When the adjutant shrugged, palms up, Santa Anna continued, "*No importa. No tiene importancia, el numero. Los muertos están muertos y se merecen estar muerto.* No matter. It is of no importance, the number. The dead are dead and deserve to be dead.

"From the beginning, this entire farce has been about *nada* but pirating the territory from us and delivering it to their American masters. To turn Tejas into *Gringolandia* while making a mockery of our laws and abusing the hospitality of our people, *alta, baja, y mediana.*

"They are like the asps of fable. After we took them to our bosom, they betrayed us, turned on us. Had I not stopped them here, now, they would have destroyed us. *¿Qué otra cosa puedo tener, eh Almonte?* What choice did I have, eh Almonte?"

"*Ninguno, mi General. Ellos te dieron ninguna.* None General. They gave you none."

"*Correcto. Eso es. Fue la voluntad de Dios. Ninguno se atreve mi culpa por hacer la voluntad de Dios.* Right. That is right. It was God's will. None dare blame me for doing God's will."

1. *The voice of flame shake wild voice from the grave....*
2. *Bones roaring all the day long....*
3. *I have put my trust in smoke....*

A dead man, perhaps, can sense an inferno, just as *the communication of the dead is tongued with fire beyond the language of the living.*

The worst was over. But was it? Really? Was the worst really over? Or was it here. Right here. Right now.

My limp, lifeless, 177 pound, five-foot-ten-inch corpse, its deadweight, was clutched at, dragged, hoisted, carried, tossed onto a tumbril (or, conceivably, oxcart) before being jounced along the ground in advance of being lifted and tossed yet again, this time onto an imbricated heap of big branches and board lumber, mesquite faggots and sawdust, the wooded weight of which, as it was stacked criss-cross upon my chest and pelvis in alternating cake-layers of corpses and cordwood, not only crushed and flattened, but kicked free a fragrance of acacia and creosote, pecan and peach and persimmon.

Arrobas of kerosene were slung up, onto, across the heap in arcs elongated as country-miles in advance of the torches being lighted and touched to.

Whuff!

This was no humane or civilized business, reducing 257 human beings to carbon. It was hard, crude, clumsy work bereft of all ceremony, respect or reverence. And it smelled poorly. The stench of the frying human fats and greases, sebums, saps and silts, the lards, lipids, lees and lanolins, residual oils, resins, tars and turpentines, pitches and petroleums, the gravies, soups and dews that 257 barbecuing human carcasses make was intolerable. Nidorous. Not of this earth. The wind itself was helpless before it, left no alternative but to hold its own breath.

Not literally, of course—I was dead, after all, I was cruciate—but the horizon appeared to me then as near at hand as it ever had, the sky as high as halos. I watched as fleshmelt, fire-hived, lifted unstitched from ossature. I listened to burst bone sift osteoblasted to cinder and soot, these crusts and tissues of heaven re-inscribing the remnants of battle ashen overhead in the chalked residues of war.

My soul, if I had one—and I believe that I may have, I was, frankly, counting upon it—passed engulfed through charred wood, ascended winch-torqued through flame-churn, before hovering, hoisted arm's length above its lick where, released, it for the briefest instant *flitted*, drifted, then....pranced, fireshookfree, head to foot. This choreography of that which once was deep within, become that which was leapt unleashed for its life out and upward, celestial as stardust.

Get light enough, find yourself en-lightened enough, flammivomous, and—damn!—you could actually....levitate!

And this felt fine. Felt *right*. To be done with it. Shed of its shadow. Risen. A-risen. Having ascended. Transcended. This life. Its pain. The beauty of pain. How impossible, such beauty! How lethal! This peace. At last. Sweet rest. Sweeter repose.

Once—but a moment ago, wasn't it? is that conceivable?—I was the Colonel in charge of this place, commanding officer of the outpost here. But now, now everyone was dead. My men to a man were dead, and I am little but rumor, embers windblown cold across a killing field while:

....terrified young men
Quick on their feet
Lob one another's skulls across
Wings of strange birds that are burning
Themselves alive.

And the outpost? The outpost I once commanded? The Alamo? The Alamo no longer matters. If it ever did. And it never did.

Martyrs seldom merit the meaning of their martyrdom, and anyone, anyone at all—today, tomorrow, the next day or day after that—can and must and will gladly die for a cause, the one they in their confusion convince themselves is worth fighting for.

In light of which, all that may matter is the morning still to come. And the one after that. And the one after that. Awakening. Emerging alive. Arising. From the dream.

Or the nightmare.

Ashes, all that faces up

(ad astra)

In the incendiary hush
A language of soot silent as cilia
Burns too bright to bear:

And then the order was issued: *¡Enciendalos! ¡Fuego ellos!*
Light 'em up! Fire 'em up!
¡Enviarlos al infierno!
Send them to hell!
And the raptors, disturbed, rose in a flock
As angry as a starving man
Deprived of his last meal

The sky has beaks
There is no slop it will not eat
Stoop to eat
                    chewing sulfur, spewing ash

(A human corpse requires five hours to combust and carbonize yielding ten pounds of coomb per carcass, its skull when it explodes uncannily resembling the blast of a Nock Volley Gun.)

Sooner or later whatever is left always is lost
Sooner or later nothing happens as it otherwise will
Sooner or later that which once was may still be occurring
Sooner or later a man is prey, quarry or prey:
                    "O god, my god, can Time, now,
                        ferry me the rest of the way?"

All the trouble we go to	*All the chaos*	*All the life*
to go on and on	*contained in the chaos*	*we try to live*
being in trouble	*of the uncontainable moment*	*in lieu of the inevitable*

Yesterday's ashes suspended in the air
Enjamb the spot (*) where a story once stopped
Text torched, tuskless, teeth bared.

* The only hope, or else despair
 Lies in the choice of pyre or pyre—
 To be redeemed from fire by fire.

Travis is a liar.

Travis is a god**damn** liar.

All his reports are lies and **damned** lies.

There are no Mexican forces there in *Bejar*.

It is only electioneering schemed by him to sustain his popularity; he grandstands, he always has been little but a grandstander.

I do not believe that he is the author of all these so-called appeals. He is not capable of such writing. He hasn't the words or the way with them. I believe they are false reports got up by the Mexicans to entice us out into the open in a faraway place where they might have their bloody way with us.

> —Texas Army Commander-in-Chief,
> Major-General Sam Houston
> to W.W. Thompson at Burnham's Crossing
> halfway between San Felipe and Gonzales
> March 8, 1836

What was is not. Not any longer. A man appears in many places at once. Bobs a moment. Disappears beneath their waves. Many waves.

Buffeted by the inscrutable surf of dates, historic dates, he loses all sense of time, of chronology and direction, of which was when and what once was, forgetting, if he ever knew, what he was supposed to remember about what incident or event or occasion corresponds to what year or whose name belongs to whose identity or where what happened is said to have occurred, fated never to know life save as the figment of a corrupt imagination.

For his is a clock wound backward. Its hands rush in reverse and he is caught there, enmeshed in its gears, trapped in its flow, hanging on for dear death, reposed contra in time. The past never is over for him. The past is his present, that present his future, and the places are each the same place—shabby, soul-less, oceanically soul-less, shorn of all *duende*.

A life always is made too little of—beached amidst the shallows, scuttled upon the shoals, brought up short of shore, incomplete and unfinished, fragmented, flindered, half-told. Bleached through to the broke white in the bone.

Death wields the upper hand. Determines the story's end. How it will end. Too soon.

What it writes is written in blood: rest in peace, rest in memory, rest in meaning, rest in such lies as survive. Because soul is the sole witness, you see. Soul alone. Soul alone is the witness.

There are no fairytales.

Back in Alabama, the Ma, upon being informed that her first-born, her eldest son, is dead, betrays or feigns to betray no surprise or other inkling of discernible emotion beyond remarking matter-of-factly, "Well, I'll wager they found no wounds in that boy's back," while the Pap, at best but half the man he once was owing to a left-hemispheric stroke suffered but the year before, musters little but a vacant, dysarthriatic stare out of which at some tortured length issues a gurged-up grotesquerie of sound, a wrenched, wretchedly garbled, arguably intelligible howl or wail that many of those present take for the word:

"Who?"

onde esta el perro? That dread damn dead pariah dog, the one that hounds me so.

I wonder. Am left to wonder. Been wondering lately. All these years later. Whether upon being shot, in that moment when the lightning spat up through the darkness from down below splitting my head apart, and I, reeling, glimpsed above me for a last lofty moment some ineluctable metallic brilliance and heard deep in my ears the crack of the thunderclaps even as I felt a sort of queer relief realizing that I had been shot and fell then against the cannon, across its caldera, that volcano, sliding slowly under it, sinking under thinking how *dingy* a way this was to die, I wonder whether as I lay there sensing the life slithering out of me like so much offal, like lava in the lack of last light looking red, blue, blue-black, wonder as I screamed and heard myself screaming and heard the echoes of my screaming return to me as they lifted out and across the courtyard in the dark caroming off the walls of the compound, that BURROW....

I wonder, did somebody, anybody at all, after it was over, all over, last word, *palabra ultima*, did someone, some Good Samaritan perhaps, one possessed of the requisite *duende*, bother to throw a dead dog down after me?

The only secret people keep, Is Immortality.
&
The only immortality, is absence.

"There is a saying here," he wrote in his diary mere hours before his murder, "what they call a refrane: *'Hay más tiempo que vida.' Which roughly means, 'There is more time, than life.'*

"It is the nature of History to take its time, for only time can tell. It may well be, as another of their refranes *goes, that* 'El embrague de la Historia no es sino un traba a la Vida,' *that 'The clutch of History is but a fetter to Life,' but come what may, I am content, as I must be, to wait upon the writing of its next, and final, stanza.*

"Time can be killed. Each of us has done our share of it. But it cannot be silenced. The poets will come. The poets will come because while there may be more time than life, there is more **duende** *than time. In that, I repose both my confidence and my faith. In time, the poets will come to weave what they will of the* SOUL *of what they alone will find here:*

Sin lagrimas, profanidades, sin gritos de la crucifixion de, solo la notica del latido de nuestra sangre, solo los susurros de huesos.

> *No tears, profanities, no cries of crucifixion,*
> *only the tidings of the beat of our blood,*
> *only the whispers of bones.*

Que se necesita para que los muertos descansan en paz?

It is easy to lose Travis when the story grows larger, to forget the individual....easy to forget the unhappiness of his life....or the hope....But it was all there in him, for he was the sum of it.....the making of him....he remained to the end what he had become....

—Archie P. McDonald, his biographer

Citations

p. 8, boldface: Jules Laforgue ("Albums")

p. 9, parenthetical in italics: Eleni Sikelianos ("At Night The Autoportrait")

p. 44, parenthetical in italics: Mei-mei Berssenbrugge ("Texas")

p. 130, in italics: William Carlos Williams ("Kora in Hell")

p. 133, ff: The section, "February 23rd," is glossed after Kafka.

p. 133, in italics: Christian Bok (*The Xenotext*)

p. 135, in italics: William Carlos Williams ("Kora in Hell")

p. 138, in italics: Lyn Hejinian ("The Distance")

p. 140, parenthetical in boldface: Clayton Eshleman ("Notes on a Visit to Le Tuc D'Audoubert" and "Navel of the Moon")

p. 184, in italics: Roy Fuller ("Death")

p. 197: W.G. Sebald ("Austerlitz"), translated by Anthea Bell, translation copyright © 2001 by Anthea Bell. Excerpt used by permission of Random House, an imprint and division of Penguin Random House LLC. All rights reserved.

p. 198, 1st line in italics: William Carlos Williams ("Kora in Hell")

p. 198, 2nd line in italics: Anne Carson ("The Beauty of the Husband")

p. 203, boldface: Robert Creeley ("Heroes")

p. 204: Paul Muldoon ("Cows")

p. 205: Samuel Beckett ("The Unnamable")

p. 205: William Carlos Williams ("Rome")

p. 206: William Gass ("Life Sentences")

p. 207: Seamus Heaney ("Nobel Lecture")

p. 208, 1st parenthetical in italics: Lucie Brock-Broido ("Uncollected Poem")

p. 208, 2nd parenthetical in italics: Gilbert Sorrentino ("A Celebration of Sorts")

p. 218, lines in boldface italics: Ronald Johnson ("ARK: The Foundations")

p. 218, phrase in italics: T.S Eliot (*Four Quartets*, "Little Gidding")

p. 219, in italics: James Wright ("A Mad Fight Song")

p. 220: Didier Cahen ("Ashes, all that faces up")

p. 222, bottom of page: T.S. Eliot (*Four Quartets*, "Little Gidding")

p. 226, 2nd-to-last line: Emily Dickinson ("Reticence")

p. 226, last line: Lyn Hejinian ("The Distance")

p. 228: Archie McDonald (*William Barret Travis: A Biography*)

Acknowledgments

While literature about the Texas Revolution and the Siege & Battle of the Alamo, as well as that inspired by such iconic figures as David Crockett, James Bowie, Sam Houston and Santa Anna, is so considerable as to constitute its own cottage industry, the inclusion here of a comprehensive bibliography of such works would be not only inappropriate, but needlessly onerous. The literature which encompasses the life entire of William Barret Travis is markedly less so.

To my knowledge there exists but a single serious biography, Archie McDonald's eponymously-titled, 200-plus page work published some 40 years ago, a scholarly effort that remained unsurpassed until William C. Davis published his monumental, meticulously documented, *Three Roads to the Alamo* (1998), a groundbreaking "multiple" biography of 22 chapters, roughly a quarter of which are devoted to Travis. As for works of fiction, *This Way Slaughter*, for all its contraventions and transmutations of historical fact, is, so far as I have been able to determine, the first to conjure Travis as its protagonist.

With respect to the Alamo itself, two works merit special mention. Mark Lemon's impeccably researched, cinematically detailed, *The Illustrated Alamo 1836: A Photographic Journey* (2008), is an invaluable resource for those interested not only in appreciating what that place may once have looked like, but in contextualizing what it felt like; it is nothing less than a five-course meal for the mind's eye. Floyd Collins's stirring *What Harvest: Poems on the Siege & Battle of the Alamo* (2011), is unquestionably the most accomplished collection of poesy and prose poetry upon the subject.

Absent the availability of the aforementioned works, it is conceivable that certain aspects of *This Way Slaughter* might have evolved somewhat differently.

It perhaps merits remarking at this point that as an author who subscribes to the dictum that, all equal, writers of fiction must refrain from "explaining" their work, I am content, for better or worse, to permit the words as written upon the page to speak for themselves. That said, I am not insensitive to the oft-voiced confusion of certain readers with respect to the mongrelized nature of a work such as this—namely, a fiction that is inspired by, yet one that aims deliberately to transcend the strictly "historical."

It may help to state, then, that any and all augmentations, variations, violations, omissions and outright contradictions of historical "fact" are both strictly of my own devising and purposefully calculated. On those occasions where History and Aesthetics, Fact and Fabrication found themselves in competition or conflict, it typically was the former that found itself during the writing obliged to defer to the latter. In so many words, it was what was up the creative sleeve that received priority over what was pulled from the historical hat.

I wish to thank Sarah Stegall for her generous support and good counsel, Bryce Milligan for both the keenness of his editorial vision and enviable sense of and unshakeable commitment to a finer craftsmanship, and Nancy Bocina for her patience, understanding and unqualified grace and graciousness absent which *This Way Slaughter* must only have expired in utero.

About the Author

Reared in the Upper Midwest, Bruce Olds has lived at various periods in New York City, Philadelphia, Baltimore, Miami and Chicago. He is the author of three award-winning works of fiction, the Pulitzer Prize nominated *The Moments Lost* (Farrar, Straus & Giroux, 2007), *Bucking the Tiger* (Farrar, Straus & Giroux, 2001) and the Pulitzer Prize Finalist, *Raising Holy Hell* (Henry Holt, 1995).

His nonfiction work has appeared in *Granta* and *American Heritage* among other publications. His book reviews have been published in the *Chicago Tribune*, the *Los Angeles Times* and the *Miami Herald*.

After working his way through college as a Teamster, Olds worked for several years at daily newspapers, first in Philadelphia, then in Baltimore, as an award-winning columnist, feature writer, and book reviewer, before leaving the business mid-career to devote himself full time to writing fiction.

His *sui generis* approach to his historical fictions—one that is genre-blurring, multi-dimensional, frankly collagist, and that privileges language and architecture over strict historicity—is, he suspects, in part the result of his having as an undergraduate studied under and been influenced by the pioneering literary Postmodernist scholar Ihab Hassan.

Olds's novel about the abolitionist John Brown, *Raising Holy Hell*, was an IMPAC Dublin Literary Award nominee, amd was named Novel of the Year by the Notable Books Council of the American Library Association. It also received the Quality Paperback Book Club's New Voices Award for Fiction. *Bucking the Tiger*, an ALA Notable Book, was adapted for the stage as "The Confessions of Doc Holliday." His third, set in turn-of-the-century Chicago and Michigan's Upper Peninsula, plumbed parts of his own family history.

The father of an adult son, Olds lives along the Atlantic Coast of northern South Carolina.

Wings Press was founded in 1975 by Joanie Whitebird and Joseph F. Lomax, both deceased, as "an informal association of artists and cultural mythologists dedicated to the preservation of the literature of the nation of Texas." Publisher, editor and designer since 1995, Bryce Milligan is honored to carry on and expand that mission to include the finest in American writing—meaning all of the Americas, without commercial considerations clouding the decision to publish or not to publish.

Wings Press produces multi-cultural books, chapbooks, ebooks, recordings and broadsides that, we hope, enlighten the human spirit and enliven the mind. Everyone ever associated with Wings has been or is a writer, and we know well that writing is a transformational art form capable of changing the world, primarily by allowing us to glimpse something of each other's souls. We believe that good writing is innovative, insightful, and interesting. But most of all it is honest. As Bob Dylan put it, "To live outside the law, you must be honest."

Likewise, Wings Press is committed to treating the planet itself as a partner. Thus the press uses as much recycled material as possible, from the paper on which the books are printed to the boxes in which they are shipped.

As Robert Dana wrote in *Against the Grain,* "Small press publishing is personal. In essence, it's a matter of personal vision, personal taste and courage, and personal friendships." Welcome to our world.

colophon

This first edition of *This Way Slaughter,* by Bruce Olds, has been printed on 55 pound Edwards Brothers "natural" paper containing a percentage of recycled fiber. Titles and dropped capitals have been set in Gunshot Rough type; the text in Adobe Caslon type. This book was designed by Bryce Milligan.

WingsPress

www.wingspress.com
Wings Press titles are distributed to the trade by the
Independent Publishers Group
www.ipgbook.com

Also available as an ebook.